Fang's

Miracle

Wolfsbane Ridge MC

Book 7

Author Marissa Ann

Copyright 2022 Marissa Ann

Credits:
Cover Design by: Don't Sweat It Graphics

ASIN:
ISBN-13: 979-8-9852360-3-3

Note From The Author

I hope you enjoy Fang's story as much as I do. When his story rushed forward inside my brain demanding to be told, it honestly left me in tears.

It does have a happy ending as all my books do so enjoy!

Chapter 1
Fang

The clubhouse is busy today with the preparations for Thanksgiving dinner tomorrow at the hospital. Our VP's ole lady started a tradition last year of cooking for the families staying in the children's wing.

"Okay, now that everyone is here, Mina has an announcement to make." Prez speaks loudly to get everyone's attention.

Looking over at his ole lady, I wait to see what is going on. This is obviously not a regular Church meeting because the women are never included in those.

"We are planning to do a secret Santa for the kids at the hospital this year. Tomorrow after all the kids and their families eat dinner, we will each draw names from a bowl. Whoever's name you draw will be who you need to buy gifts for." She looks at the crowd of faces until she stops at mine. "Real gifts Fang."

I smile lopsidedly at her, not saying a word. She already knows me too well. Although I still haven't gotten even with her and the other girls for the frog fiasco a few years back when I was still a prospect. I've gotta admit it was pretty fucking epic what those women planned and executed.

"Don't forget that everyone needs to be on time tomorrow. Those of you that are helping get the food there need to be at Bella's Brew no later than ten a.m. The rest of you should be here to ride to the hospital in formation." Prez says before calling the impromptu meeting to a close.

Walking over to the bar, I spot Dane sitting on a stool with a beer in his hand.

"Getting started kind of early, huh?" I say, taking the seat next to him.

He shrugs his shoulders, "Its five o'clock somewhere."

Signaling to the prospect manning the bar to bring me a cold one, I look back at Dane. He seems to be lost in thought more and more these days.

I've known him for a long time so I know the holidays are a huge problem for him. He's never told me all the details; I just know it has something to do with his family that live back east. Although this year he seems a little worse for wear.

"You okay, man?" I finally break the silence.

"Just been thinking a lot. About family and shit." He looks around the room at the other brothers.

Looking over at the brothers who are married now, some with kids, I too feel a small ache of wanting what they have.

"We'll find what they have one day." I say.

"Fuck. Listen at us. Sounding like emotional ass women." He makes a face.

I laugh, "You started the shit."

"Come on, we gotta go do some manly shit to get our man card back." We stand up, grabbing what's left of our beers, leaving through the front door.

Autumn

Sitting here on the bench outside the hospital, I can't stop the lone tear that slips down my face.

I left Dr. Ortez's office about ten minutes ago after he told me that Olivia's cancer is progressing to the point that we need a bone marrow transplant.

That wouldn't be a problem if a donor was easily found but that is not the case.

The most likely candidate would be a family member but we don't have anyone except each other. So getting her on the registry and hoping to find a match is the only hope we have.

Drying my face off, I head back inside to Livie's room, hoping she won't be able to tell that I've been crying.

Walking into her room, I see that she is sitting up on her bed playing the video game one of the nurses gave to her when she got admitted last week.

She smiles as I walk into the room. "Hey, mommy, where've you been? You missed all the motorcycles!" She says with huge eyes.

"I heard them. They were loud." I smile at her excitement.

"They were so cool! The nurse says they are friends of Dr. Ortez and that he also rides a motorcycle. Do you think he would take me for a ride?" She's talking so fast, her sentences run together making me laugh.

"Maybe you can ask him later. Before we head down to the cafeteria, I need to talk to you a minute about what Dr. Ortez had to talk to me about." I sit on the edge of her bed with my heart pounding unsure exactly how to tell an eight year old that she needs a transplant.

"We aren't leaving the hospital, are we?" She huffs, lying back against her pillows.

"Not for a while sweetheart. Remember when we talked about what would happen if you needed a donor?" I ask gently.

"I remember. Dr. Ortez said I would have to stay in the hospital for a really long time." She looks at me with so much trust it breaks my heart.

What will I do if we can't find a match in time? How will I explain to my daughter that she could possibly die?

Holding even more tears at bay, I say, "Come on. Let's go eat." I smile standing up next to her bed.

"You think they'll have pie?" She hops up with excitement yet again as if we were not just talking about a longer stay in the hospital.

"Is pie the only thing you want?" I laugh at her.

"Nope. I want some ham with my pie." She nods her head, grabbing my hand as we walk out of the room.

Fang

After helping to set up all the tables with the food, I head outside to a bench that is under a gazebo hoping for a few minutes alone.

Pulling out a pack of smokes, I light one up taking a huge drag, filling my lungs with smoke. The only times I ever smoke is on days that the memories of my baby brother take over my brain.

Being around the kids today at the hospital has brought back memories of him that I try to hide deep inside.

"Those are bad for you, ya know?" A little voice from behind me causes me to jump.

Putting it out, I turn around to see a tiny little girl bundled up in her jacket against the cold wind sitting on the bench I was hoping to pass a little time on.

"I don't do it often." I finally say in reference to the cigarette she caught me with. "What are you doing out here alone?" I look around for her parents but don't see any one.

"Momma is talking with Dr. Ortez again." She rolls her eyes, swinging her legs back and forth.

Looking closely at her, she doesn't look sick but I know that's not an indication that she's not. My little brother didn't look sick either.

"So what's your name munchkin?" I smile when she gives me a look for calling her that.

"Well, it's not Munchkin." She huffs. "My name is Olivia."

Smiling with what I'm about to do, "Olivia is a beautiful name but I think I like Munchkin better."

"Now I know why momma says boys are weird and that I should stay away from them." She shakes her head, never cracking a smile. "What do I call you? Smoke Man?" She says with a grin as I laugh.

"My friends call me Fang." I offer her my hand which she shakes.

"Fang is a weird name. Do you have vampire teeth or something?" She narrows her eyes, looking towards my mouth.

"If I said yes, could we still be friends?" I ask as seriously as I can.

She seems to think about it for a minute before answering. "If you were a vampire and you bit me, would that get rid of my cancer?" Her eyes finally look up into my own and I am struck by the seriousness her dark brown eyes convey.

As I turn her question over in my head, my heart beats harder within my chest knowing that I need to be extremely careful with how I answer her. Right now is not the time for my usual playful nature.

Sitting down next to her, I place my elbows on my knees and look directly back at her.

"I don't know that much about vampire's kiddo but I do know doctors. If there's a way, they will find it."

She looks hard at me for several long minutes as she thinks over what I said before sitting back on the bench.

"I like you Fang." She smiles.

"I like you too, Livie." I respond back with my own grin.

"That's what my mom calls me. Unless she's upset, then she calls me Olivia." She giggles.

"I think Olivia is a beautiful name for a very beautiful little girl." I reach over, putting her tiny hand in my own, giving it a small squeeze.

We sit just like that, lost in our own thoughts for several long minutes until someone else comes out the hospital door.

"Olivia!" We hear her yell, both turning towards her voice.

"Uh oh." Livie and I say at the same time before we start to laugh.

Hopefully the woman coming towards us doesn't plan to eat me alive for hanging out with her little girl.

Autumn

Looking out the glass doors and seeing Livie sitting with some strange man made my throat squeeze up.

Yelling her name as I came out the door didn't seem to faze either one of them because they both broke out into hysterical laughter.

By the time I get to the gazebo where they are both sitting, their laughter has started to fade.

Looking Olivia over first, as is my habit these days, I don't pay the man very much attention.

"It's too cold for you to be out here little lady." I say, kneeling down in front of her.

"I got my coat momma." She giggles. "This is my new friend Fang."

"Fang?" I look over quickly to the man still sitting on the bench.

This close I can see he is a very handsome man, almost too handsome. I realize I've been staring too long when he begins to grin at me and I can feel my face start to flush with embarrassment.

Slightly clearing my throat, I hold my hand out to him.

"I'm Autumn, Olivia's mom. It's nice to meet you." I say, waiting for his hand to shake my own.

I'm not prepared for the electricity that zaps up my arm at first contact with him. I can tell that he felt it too by the slight widening of his eyes.

"Nice to meet you ma'am." He grins again.

Polite and manners, that's rare in most of the men I've met. I think to myself.

"I should get back inside and help my friends." He looks back at the hospital doors before turning back to us.

"Your friends?" I ask, confused.

"Yeah. My club is the one holding the Thanksgiving dinner inside for all the kids. You two should make sure you come in for some food."

He looks over at Olivia directly with another huge grin just for her that causes my heart to beat quickly. No one has ever looked at my daughter in such a way. Most of the men I've tried to date over the years would always see her as a nuisance.

"Is there pie?" Olivia stands up from the bench.

"Absolutely the best pie in the world. One of the ole ladies in the club owns Bella's Brew. Have you ever been there?" He asks her.

Neither of them pays me any mind as they begin walking with each other back towards the hospital doors, chatting the entire way.

I finally pick up my pace, jogging a little to catch up with them.

Fang

Helping Livie fill her plate with all the things she wants to eat, I watch her mother out of the corner of my eye. She seems at a loss for the way that I engage with her daughter.

It's sad to think of what kind of men have caused her to behave in such a way. I couldn't imagine ever treating a child badly. They are the greatest gifts, even if they are not your own.

I lead them both towards a table in the corner, sitting Olivia's food in front of one of the chairs.

We all eat in silence, watching everyone else move around the room talking to each other.

"There's a whole bunch of you. Are they your family?" Olivia asks with awe, scanning the room with her eyes.

Looking around myself, I realize that she is right. There are a lot of us in the club and we all consider each other family.

"We are family because we choose to be family." I answer.

"What do you mean?" Autumn asks.

"When you become part of the club, you swear to put the club family first because we all are more like family than our blood family is. Some of the guys join up simply because they are looking for that family dynamic. It's something they never had with their real families." I shrug my shoulders hoping that I explained it well enough for her to understand.

"So you guys adopted each other?" Olivia asks and I can't stop my smile in her direction.

Only a child could put it so simply but it still hit the mark dead on.

"Exactly."

She grins at me, taking a huge bite of her chocolate pie and I do the same. Both of us are trying hard to not let any fall out of our mouths as we chew.

Autumn

"Fang, are you corrupting one of these kids already?" A beautiful dark haired woman stops next to our table with her hand on her hip.

I feel a slight twinge in my chest at the thought that this woman might be slightly more important to Fang than just family. Perhaps a wife or girlfriend.

"You offend me Mina. I would never do such a thing." He gasps with mock shock, Olivia starts to giggle.

The dark haired woman turns her smile my way.

"Hello, I'm Mina, this big lugs sister." She jerks her thumb his way.

At her admission, the breath I hadn't realized I had been holding let's go of my lungs in time to find my own manners.

"My name is Autumn and that's my daughter Olivia." I smile back at her.

"If he gives you any trouble over here do not hesitate to let me know and I will send someone to handle him." She tries to say it with a straight face but we all can see the twinkle in her eye.

"Seriously Mina, I'm being an angel today which is more than I can say for Dane, who seems to be about to start a food fight." At Fang's words, Mina gasps, turning towards the commotion in the middle of the room and taking off in that direction.

Fang laughs as he watches her stride up to another man, grabbing him by the ear like a two year old child.

The man in question is just as big as Fang and could easily cast Mina to the side. Instead of doing so though, he seems to be pleading with her to let his ear go.

"He's gonna be feeling that tomorrow." Fang laughs around another bite of pie.

Olivia is also watching the scene across the room with interest, laughing along with Fang.

"She's not afraid of any of you." I say it like a statement although I'm asking a question.

"Why would she be? She's the Queen bee in our club plus we know our manners. Women should never be hurt in any way. Neither should kids." He smiles down at Livie.

She's now looking up at him with eyes that seem to scream that she thinks he's the greatest thing she has ever seen in her short little life.

My heart squeezes tighter inside my chest.

Chapter 2
Fang

A week after Thanksgiving I find myself making my way back to the hospital to visit with Olivia.

I gave her my number before the club left that day and she's made it a habit to call me after her mother has fallen asleep late at night.

We usually talk about all kinds of things until she is sleepy enough to fall asleep herself. The kid has a wicked sense of humor much like my own.

She's been trying to help me to devise a plan to get the women back for the frogs. I, of course, left out several details of the reason for the frogs. Can't have her having nightmares or something like all of a sudden being scared of me now.

I look forward to our nightly talks. I especially like the talks where she shares even more information about herself and her mother.

The things they have both gone through before coming here makes the caveman inside of me roar with the need to gather them both up and protect them for the rest of their lives.

"Fang, what are you doing here?" I hear as soon as I walk through the hospital doors.

"Doc." I nod in his direction. "I thought I would visit Olivia for a bit today but I wanted to talk to you first." I say.

"Of course, come into my office." He says, leading the way into the room. "Now what can I help you with?" He looks at me waiting.

"Livie said that she would be going through chemo again and some other medications that would mean she would have to be put into what she called a safe room. Can you clarify all that for me please?" I sit down in the chair in front of his desk.

At first he just looks at me, most likely wondering why I am getting so attached to this little girl. Very few within the club know about my baby brother and I am hoping that Doc will just keep his mouth shut.

"Well, the straightforward explanation is that she needs a bone marrow transplant but while we have her on the transplant list waiting for a match, the chances of that are very slim. So to try and combat the rapidly growing cancer cells we are once again trying an aggressive chemotherapy treatment. She'll need to be in what is called a clean room so that germs stay out. Even a small cold could kill her." He waits for me to digest this information.

"How does one find out if they can be a donor?" I ask without thinking about it.

"Fang, this isn't something you rush into. Being a bone marrow donor is an amazing thing. But it hurts. A lot. It would take you a while to completely heal." He tries explaining it all to me but I've already made up my mind without needing time to think it over.

I shake my head at him until he stops talking. "I don't care Doc. Run whatever tests you need to run. I want to know if I can be her donor." I start to stand up.

"The chances of you being specifically Olivia's match is super slim, Fang." He gets up from his desk.

"Doc, I can't explain it. It's something I truly feel deep inside. I'm going to be her match. Set it up please." I stare into his eyes trying to let him see just how important to me this is.

He finally shakes his head in the affirmative. "Thanks Doc. One more thing, is she still okay to go out to lunch today for a bit? We shouldn't be gone long but I thought it would do her good before she is forced to stay in the clean room." I wait for his answer before I walk out of his office in search of Livie and Autumn.

As I walk around a corner, I see the two of them looking out the window at the end of the hall. The way the sunlight shines through on the two of them puts a knot in my chest.

"Ladies." I say, getting their attention.

"Fang!" Livie yells, running straight into my legs, wrapping her arms around me.

As I raise my smiling face to look up at her mother, the look she's giving me causes an overwhelming urge in me to kiss her pouty lips.

The thought puts a playful grin on my face and I watch as her face turns a slight red. Hopefully she was thinking the same thing that I was.

Autumn

I'm surprised at my interest in this man. There hasn't been anyone in a really long time that has grabbed my attention like he has.

To look at him you wouldn't know there was a sweet man underneath. One that has no problem having entire serious conversations about a talking sponge that lives under the sea.

Since spending time with him at Thanksgiving I know that he and Livie have been having nightly phone conversations about all kinds of things.

The one they had two nights ago was the one that really pulled at my heart and left me quietly sobbing into my pillow without giving myself away.

Instead of coming to me to discuss death and what happens after, my sweet little girl talked with a man we've only known a short little while.

I'm not exactly sure how he answered her questions but it must have eased her little mind more than I ever could have.

It wasn't long before they were back giggling about making plans that may or may not have to do with spiders.

I have no idea what kind of plans they've made with that and I'm not entirely sure I really want to know. Just as long as it has nothing to do with me because I will absolutely flip out if a spider gets within a foot of me.

"I wanted to see if the two of you wanted to go grab lunch at Bella's Brew today." Fang asks, looking to me for an answer.

"Please momma?" Olivia looks up to me with her beautiful dark eyes, pleadingly.

"I don't know. We should probably ask Dr. Ortez first and make sure it's okay." I should probably say no but I don't want to stop Livie from a small outing that could possibly be her last for quite some time.

"I already cleared it with him. He said it would be fine for us to go to lunch then come right back afterward." He points that sexy ass grin my way again.

Seriously, men like him should not exist. Sexy as hell and able to turn most women on with only a grin. It just isn't fair.

Shaking my head to clear my thoughts, I look back at him and can tell he probably knows exactly what he's doing to me.

"Okay. Let's go eat some lunch." I answer, looking to Olivia to keep my eyes off the man now standing a little bit too close.

"Yes!" Olivia jumps up and down in excitement. "I want a super huge hamburger!" She announces, grabbing mine and Fang's hand with each of her own.

We walked out of the hospital connected like that. To anyone looking on, we looked like any other family. The pang in my chest squeezes even tighter.

Fang

Lunch with the girls was a lot of fun. Several of the brothers and their families were there as well so they got to meet quite a few people.

All the brothers of course gave me a look that clearly said there would be questions later as to what I was doing.

Honestly, I don't know what I'm doing. All I know is that I enjoy their company and Autumn is absolutely the most beautiful woman I have ever laid eyes on.

I made sure to get her cell number this time so that I could talk to her directly.

When I dropped them back off at the hospital, I knew they would be setting up the clean room for Olivia to start staying in.

Wanting to check in before I go to sleep, I pick up my phone and text Autumn.

Me: Hey. How is she?
Autumn: She's not happy about it because she thought I would be staying in the room with her.
Me: You're Not?
Autumn: No. It's not allowed.
Me: Then where are you staying?

I watch the dots come on then disappear several times and I wonder if she's going to give me an answer. Finally my phone pings and I snatch it up quickly.

Autumn: I'm heading to the motel on the other side of town.

My brows draw together as I think of the motel she's speaking of. It's full of all kinds of riffraff that she certainly shouldn't be in the middle of.

Making a quick decision, I shoot her a text telling her I would be there in fifteen minutes, to wait for me by the hospital doors.

I don't wait for her to reply back as I grab the keys to the cage I only ever drive in the winter and head out into the snow.

It actually takes me twenty minutes to get back to the hospital because of how much snow has accumulated on the roads.

Pulling into the parking area, I see her through the glass doors looking out into the night. Putting the SUV into park, I get out, walking toward her as she steps outside the doors.

She gives me a questioning look as I pick up her bag, slinging it over my shoulder.

"Where are we going?" She asks, getting to the truck.

"Our club owns some cabins just up the mountain a little piece." I answer, getting into the driver side and turning up the heat.

She gets in on her side, shutting the door but still looking at me like I've lost my mind.

"Most of the cabins are full but I can let you stay in mine and I'll stay at the club house if it makes you more comfortable not having me there." I explain, pulling the truck out onto the road.

"I don't want to put you out of your own house." She breathes out.

"It's not a big deal. I always have a room at the club in case I ever want to stay over there. The cabin is new. We only just built mine earlier this year." I rush out hoping she doesn't fight me on it.

I don't have to stay there with her although I am hoping she wants me to stay. I feel connected to her in a way that I've never felt to a woman before.

Don't even get me started on the feelings I have for her sweet little girl. I would love to have a daughter exactly like her one day. I wonder if she would let me claim her anyway.

"So, you okay with this?" I ask, turning onto the mountain road that heads to Wolf's Ridge.

"Yes. Thank you. But I don't want to put you out. Do you have a couch or extra bedroom or something?" She whispers. Even though it is dark I can guess that her face is turning red. I can't stop the grin that gives me or the jerk behind my zipper.

"There's two bedrooms, so there's plenty of room for us both." I answer, coming to a stop in front of the cabin steps.

Autumn

We pull up to a beautiful cabin with a wrap around porch that I am sure is amazing to see in the light of day.

My heart hammers in my chest as we climb the stairs walking through the door.

The inside is amazing with high ceilings and large open spaces. The kitchen is huge with granite counter tops and top of the line appliances.

"It's beautiful." I whisper.

"Yes, you certainly are." His whispered voice has me turning in his direction but he's already turning away. "You can take the bedroom on the left." He continues through the room, setting my bag just inside.

"The bathroom is at the end of the hall. Should be plenty of towels and things in there. Extra toothbrushes in the drawer if you need one." He turns back my way, looking at me from head to toe.

He bites his lower lip and I shiver at the thought of biting it myself. I know he notices when his grin returns to his face.

"Have you eaten? I can warm you up some spaghetti. Mina dropped it off while I was gone earlier." He says.

My stomach grumbles at the thought of food. I smile back at him. "That would be great, thank you."

"No problem. Get comfortable. I'll have the table set when you get out of the shower." With his last word, he bites his lip again.

Turning away quickly, I go into the bedroom getting what I will need from my bag and head straight into the bathroom.

I turn the water on, and then stare at my reflection in the mirror for long moments willing my body to calm down.

By the time I finish my shower, I'm soaking wet in a completely needy way and wondering how I'm ever going to be able to control my body's reaction to this man while staying under the same roof.

I'm even more certain that I won't be able to, when I walk back into the kitchen after my shower and the sexy ass man is wearing nothing but a pair of shorts.

He's covered in amazing tattoos that accentuate the muscles he seems to have all over his entire body. Simply put, the man is a glorious piece of art. One I want to lick.

I must have sighed, alerting him to my presence as he begins speaking to me before ever turning around.

Fang

"Keep staring at me like that and I won't be responsible for what I do." I say, turning around to look at her.

Her hair is still wet from her shower and what little makeup she had on earlier is completely gone from her face.

She's beautiful as hell without it. Her cheeks are bright red, most likely from being caught staring at me. Deciding to let her off the hook a little more easily, I turn toward the table I've set for us.

"Come eat. Then we can watch a movie or something if you want to." Taking my seat, I wait for her to sit as well before passing her the bread.

"This smells so good." She sighs, filling her plate.

"I think it's the best spaghetti around if you ask me. Bella is an amazing cook." I answer, filling my own.

"I thought you said Mina brought it over?" She looks over at me with surprise.

"She did but it's definitely from Bella's." I watch as she takes a bite, letting out a small hum as the taste fills her mouth.

I feel my cock jump in my shorts watching her mouth.

I'd love to know what it would feel like having her wrapped around me as she hummed.

Adjusting myself discreetly, I ask her about where she moved from.

"Anchorage actually. Our doctor there referred Olivia to Dr. Ortez. Claimed he was the best. So we packed up and here we are." She shrugs.

"What about Olivia's father?" I ask unexpectedly.

I've wondered more than once where her father could possibly be. If she were mine, I'd be right next to her through it all.

"Um, could we not bring him up please?" She looks down at her plate.

"I'm sorry. Wasn't trying to upset you." I apologize.

"He's just a jackass is all. He doesn't actually care about her but he can't get out of being her father without it looking badly on him in his office." She stabs her fork into her noodles.

"One of those then." I grit out, squeezing my hand around my own fork. Good thing it's not glass, it would break.

"Yep. So, if you don't mind, I'd rather not talk about him. I don't bring him up around Livie so I don't upset her." She admits.

We finish our meals in relative silence, both standing up at the same time to clear the table.

We actually work very well together cleaning up. She seemed to know exactly where all the dishes should go.

"Want to watch a movie?" I ask when we are finished.

"Sure." She blushes again.

We take a seat on the couch in the living room and I grab the remote scrolling through the movies listed on it.

Finding one I think she would enjoy, I start it then get up grabbing a blanket from the hall closet before turning the overhead light off.

Handing it to her, she covers herself up with a grateful smile, leaning back into the corner of the couch.

If she leans any further away she might actually fall off into the floor.

Getting comfortable on my own end, I prop my feet up onto the coffee table.

After an hour of the movie she begins to move around as if uncomfortable and I've noticed she's gotten a little closer.

Not saying a word, I put my arm around her shoulder, pulling her over toward me.

Her eyes widen slightly and I feel her breathing kick up before she relaxes against me.

We both fall asleep before the movie ever ends.

Chapter 3
Autumn

That first night at Fang's cabin, we both fell asleep on the couch and somehow wound up tangled around each other in the night.

After that, I've made sure to not fall asleep on the couch with him again although my body seems to hate me for it.

I've gotten to know him more though when we sit together each night for dinner. The man is an enigma. I never would have thought he could be so kind or thoughtful.

The second night I was there, he stopped at a store after picking me up from the hospital so I could buy some things that a woman would need.

Actually, he called it "women's shit". I can't believe he actually walked down the tampon aisle with me without freaking out as most men do.

He even helped me read the boxes to be sure I got a box that was hypoallergenic.

Ever since, all I can think about is climbing his ass like a tree and hanging on like a monkey.

"Hey." I jump at the sound of his voice behind me. I'm so very glad he can't read minds.

Turning away from the coffee pot, I give him a questioning look.

"One of the guys is going to pick me up so you can take the SUV to the hospital." He hands me a set of keys.

"You sure you won't need it today?"

"Nah. I'm helping them unload a trailer of hay over at Wolf's Landing. I'll get a ride over to the hospital when we finish up." That sexy grin of his back. The one that makes me think he's imagining me naked while he talks about normal things.

"Okay." I sigh once I break eye contact with him.

"Tell the munchkin I said hello." He says, stepping closer and kissing the top of my head.

He looks surprised at himself for doing so. I'm fairly sure that my face shows the same surprise as well. With one quicker grin, he walks away.

I've been in the hospital room with Livie for several hours now. She's more sullen today and very moody. Only answering questions with one word.

And the eye rolling. Did I mention the eye rolling? She's done it no less than twenty times over the past hour and I'm having a really hard time biting my tongue.

"Christmas is only a little over a week away. Have you decided yet what you want from Santa?" I ask Livie through my mask.

"To make a snowman." She huffs, still looking out the window in her room.

"I'm so sorry sweetheart. How are you feeling with the medicine they have you on?" I rub her hair with my gloved covered hand.

I hate not being able to really touch her. To give her all the hugs and kisses a little girl needs from her mommy.

"She only gets sick the first couple hours after treatment." Dr. Ortez says coming through the door.

Olivia never turns away from the window but I turn to him, giving him a polite smile as he moves further into the room.

"Can Fang visit today?" Livie asks.

She asks every day although the answer has been no since being placed into this room. The most he's been able to do is talk to her through the glass door without actually coming in.

"Yes. He can actually." Dr. Ortez answers.

Livie swings around with wide eyes. "Really?" At the shake of his head, she bounces on the balls of her feet. "Can you call him momma?"

Before I can answer, Dr. Ortez speaks up.

"He actually should already be on his way here. I called him before I came to your room." He smiles brightly at her.

"Oh I can't wait. He's my bestest friend!" She exclaims. I can't help the watery smile I give her. It takes so very little to make her so very happy. She's an absolute gift from God as far as I'm concerned.

"Livie, I'm going to talk with your mom for just a bit but I'll send her back shortly." He says, motioning for me to follow him outside the room.

My heart kicks up at what this might be about. I hope it's not yet another setback for her condition. We can't take any more setbacks.

Following him, we make our way to his office. It must be something truly serious that he doesn't want others to hear.

My tears are falling before I ever make it to the chair in front of his desk.

"Hey, what's wrong?" He pats my shoulder, handing me a tissue.

"Something's gone wrong right? That's why you've brought me to your office to talk?" I ask through my sobs.

"No. No, that's not it at all." He shakes his head, still patting my shoulder.

"It's not?" I wipe my nose.

"No. It's not. I actually have some very good news." He goes around to his chair taking a seat, shuffling the papers around on his desk. "Here you go." He hands me a few documents.

I sit there trying to make sense of what I'm reading.

"What?" My brows draw together with my question. "Am I reading this right?"

"We found a donor." He says with a huge smile.

The water works start all over again but for a different reason.

Fang

Doc called me earlier asking me to come to the hospital so as soon as we unloaded the last bale into the barn; I got my VP to give me a ride into town.

"What's going on with you? You've been pretty tight lipped about the woman you've had staying at your cabin the last couple weeks." Blade asks as we turn onto the road.

"I'm helping her out. Her little girl is one of Doc's patients." I look out the window at the snow on the ground. Luckily there hasn't been so much that the roads are impassable.

"Terminal?" He asks.

"Could be, if she doesn't find a bone marrow donor." My chest hurts at the thought of the world losing such a sweet little girl.

"That sucks man. They say finding a donor for that is truly hard."

"I asked Doc to test me." I say quickly.

"No shit?" He says, looking over at me with drawn brows.

I can tell I surprised him with that bit of information.

"Yeah. I can't explain it but I feel that we are a match." I move around in my seat, feeling uncomfortable.

"This have anything to do with the thoughts of your brother?" He asks.

"Why would it?" I growl. The few that know about Ricky, know that I don't like talking about it.

"You can't keep blaming yourself man. You were only a kid." He sighs, turning into the hospital parking lot.

"But we were a match, Blade. One of my kidneys could have saved him!" I shouldn't take my anger out on him but I can't seem to help myself.

"And it would have also given you only a half life as well! Your parents did what they thought was best for you both." He murmurs, coming to a stop in front of the doors.

Not saying another word to him, I get out, slamming the truck door as I walk away.

Going straight to Doc's office, I find him sitting behind his desk.

"There you are." He greets me as I take a seat across from him.

"Is something wrong with Olivia?" I ask right away.

He shakes his head, "No. She's doing very well. You can actually visit her today in her room. But that's not why I asked you to come in." He hands me a stack of papers.

"What's all this?" I ask, scanning through them.

"You are definitely a match with Olivia. Not a perfect match but still enough that it could

43

work in her favor. Possibly even put her in remission." He says.

"That's fucking awesome!" I exclaim, sitting up to look closer at the paperwork he handed me. "So when can we get this done?" I ask.

"After I get you to sign all the necessary paperwork, we can have it on the schedule for next Friday." He says.

"Christmas Eve?" My brows draw together at the thought of her getting what she needs in time for Christmas. A miracle.

"Just sign all these documents here and I'll get everything set up." He hands me another stack of papers and a pen.

After signing what felt like my entire life away, I hand it all back to him with a smile on my face.

"Just one thing though Doc, I don't want either of them to know it's me just yet." He looks at me seriously for a few minutes.

"That's actually not a problem because of patient confidentiality and all that mess." He shrugs his shoulders.

"Thanks." I grunt, walking out of his office.

Getting to the nurses station, I let them point me to where I need to wash up, donning a paper gown and gloves.

I spot Olivia and Autumn through the door with their backs turned toward me so I quietly slip inside without either of them hearing me.

"Will it hurt?" I hear Olivia ask her mother.

"It shouldn't be too bad. Dr. Ortez would never allow anything to hurt you. Neither would I." She answers, running her hand down Livie's hair.

"Me either." I say, causing them both to gasp and turn around quickly.

"Fang!" Livie yells her whole face lighting up with her smile.

She runs to me wrapping her tiny arms around my waist.

"How are you doing, Munchkin?" I murmur, holding her tight.

She pulls back, looking me straight in the eyes, narrowing her own.

"I'm doing great. What about you, Smokeman?" her eyes, then holds up one brow without cracking a smile.

I can't help the laugh that escapes my mouth. This child is the greatest.

Autumn

Fang and I stopped to pick up some pasta from Bella's Brew on the way home. Instead of sitting at the table like we normally do, we are sitting on the couch next to each other watching a Christmas special.

"These types of shows always make me cry like a baby." I wipe a lone tear off my face before taking another bite.

"I won't tell anyone that you cried into your linguine." He laughs as I elbow him in the ribs.

After finishing our plates, we set them on the coffee table. That's when I notice he's staring at me.

"What?" I finally ask self conscious all of a sudden.

"You have a little something…" He says, lifting his finger to the side of my mouth. "Here." He wipes it off, sticking his finger into his own mouth.

My breathing kicks up, unable to look away from him. From those gorgeous dark eyes looking so intently at me.

"You are so fucking beautiful." He whispers, leaning close enough that I feel his breath on my lips.

"I'm going to kiss you now." He whispers even closer than before.

All I can do is barely let out a moan in answer before his mouth takes over my own.

He draws me in closer, pressing his hand into my back. My breasts tighten up at the feeling of him through my shirt and I know I am already soaking wet for this man.

Pulling back, he holds my face in his hands, breathing hard.

"I want to hold you up against the nearest wall and fuck you until you scream my name." He growls.

Oh God, do I want that too.

"What is your name?" I finally manage to get out through my now kiss swollen lips.

He begins to laugh, laying his forehead to my own.

"Jarod. My real name is Jarod." He finally answers. "But no one but you knows that. Well, and my family."

"Thank you for telling me." I smile.

He stands, pulling me up with him and walking towards his room. I let him lead me inside, shutting the door behind us.

I stand at the foot of his bed not moving as he holds eye contact with me. Reaching up, he pulls my shirt over my head revealing my white lace bra.

"So beautiful." He murmurs, running his fingers across the bra stimulating my nipple beneath. When I gasp, he moves to the other side.

He slowly moves up my arms, pulling the straps of my bra back down until my breasts pop free. Holding my eyes with his, he lowers his head sucking my right nipple into his mouth.

I throw my head back as a moan more guttural than I have ever heard crawls up the back of my throat. Throwing my hands around his head, I hold him to my breast afraid he will stop.

Never letting go with his mouth, his hands find their way to my pants, shoving them down my legs in one fast motion, exposing my center to the cool air around us.

Finally letting go of my nipple with a gentle bite first, he pushes me back until I fall onto the bed.

He jerks off his shorts quickly before slowly crawling up the bed to me.

He licks his way up my calf, moving back and forth between both legs. My thighs begin to quiver as he gets closer to my center that is begging for attention.

"Fuck, that's sexy." I feel his breath on my core as he speaks.

Before I can utter a word, his lips suck my clit into his mouth.

"Oh, fuck!" I yell, grabbing his head with my hands.

He sucks even harder, a few seconds later I feel his fingers pushing into my wet heat and I explode into his mouth with a gasp.

When I'm finally able to open my eyes, he's crawling up the rest of my body. He grabs a condom from the nightstand, slipping it on with a grin in my direction.

I flip us both until I am on top of him. His brows draw together in question but I reach for his swollen member, lining him up with my entrance.

Slowly, I sink down onto him until I am fully seated and can feel him deeper than I have ever felt anyone before.

Holding his eyes with mine, I begin a slow rhythm. I'm once again climbing closer to an orgasm each time I feel him hitting that spot so deep inside.

He grabs my hips, taking more control, slamming me down on him as he jerks upward into me.

"Oh fuck yes, Jerod. Just like that. Mmm." I moan.

"You feel so good baby. Come for me." He whispers, taking my mouth for a deep kiss.

We both come hard, me screaming into his mouth and him moaning into mine.

Chapter 4
Fang

"You're seriously doing this shit then?" Dane asks, shaking his head at me.

"Yes, I'm serious. Look it's not that big of a deal on my part. It'll just take a bit for me to heal up from it." I look to Timber, my Prez, who has his brows drawn down the way he does when he's thinking shit over.

"What you're doing is a very noble thing, Fang. There's no question about that. You should have given us more notice than the day of. I'll call Mina and we'll be at the hospital before they take you back." Prez steeples his hands together, looking around the room at each of the guys one by one.

No one will speak against it now that he's made it apparent that he supports my decision.

While we are all grown, the club comes first and that means that we take everything to the Prez first. Even the things that are personal.

"You guys plan to come?" I ask with surprise.

"You're family, man. Of course we will be there!" Blade grins at me as if I have sprouted two heads.

"What time is it scheduled for?" Blood asks, checking the time.

"Four this afternoon." I answer.

"Good. That gives us time to get everyone together." Prez stands up from the table, heading to the door as he dials Mina's number.

Looking around at all the guys, my chest swells with pride at my family. They may not share my blood but they are more family to me than anyone else in the world.

"Good thing it wasn't scheduled for tomorrow. I don't think I could have picked your ass over Christmas dinner." Wrench says loudly as everyone begins to laugh and agree with him.

"You'd pick a ham over your brother? That's just wrong!" I shake my head in disgust, another round of laughing ensues.

Autumn

I've been pacing the floor for the last hour wondering where Fang is. He promised to be here in time but I've yet to see him.

The past week with him has been pretty amazing. We'd get up every morning, have coffee, he'd drop me off at the hospital then go to work.

Soon as he got off, he'd come to the hospital and spend time with me and Olivia before we would go home together.

Once there, we'd come together explosively before passing out in each other's arms just to wake the next morning and do it all again.

"We have to take her back now. It's time." Dr. Ortez startles me from my thoughts.

"Um. Okay." I look up and down the hallway. "Have you seen Fang? He was supposed to be here." I ask, tears beginning to fill my eyes.

"Autumn?" I hear a woman's voice from beside me.

Turning in that direction, I recognize Mina who I'd met a few times since Thanksgiving.

"Do you want to come wait with us?" She points down the hall to a waiting room that looks completely full of bikers.

My confusion must show on my face as she looks at me with eyes that widen.

"He didn't tell her, did he?" She looks to Dr. Ortez who shakes his head no.

"Tell me what?" I ask, putting my hands on my hips, getting more frustrated by the minute.

"Fang is the donor. They've already taken him back to prep him." At her words, my heart feels like it's going to explode from my chest.

"Why would he not tell me something like that?" I whisper, unable to catch my breath.

"Men can be assholes." She shrugs her shoulders, rolling her eyes and I can't contain my laughter that bubbles out of me.

A large man walks up, putting his arm around Mina so I assume this to be Timber. The president of the Wolfsbane Ridge MC.

"Is she okay?" He asks seriously and I laugh even harder at the look on his face. He probably thinks I'm crazy as a loon.

"We were just talking about men being assholes." Mina states simply.

"Hey!" He looks at her sternly.

"It's the truth. But I do love you." She smiles, leaning in for a kiss. She looks back at me, raising her brow. "Ready to go meet the rest of the club?"

"Yeah." I sigh, stepping forward. "But just so you know I might kill him. After I kiss him for saving Olivia of course."

"Of course. And we other club ladies just might help you too." She looks over at Timber as we walk down the hall, then leans slightly closer to whisper to me. "Did Fang ever tell you about the frog fiasco?"

"Mina. Do not corrupt her!" Timber growls from beside her.

"Frog fiasco?" I ask, looking between the two.

"Tell you later." She whispers back with a wink.

Hooking her arm through mine, Mina pulls me towards the surgery waiting area.

"So tell me what is going to happen." she ask.

"They'll put Fang to sleep then use needles to extract the marrow from his pelvic bone. It should only take about an hour, and then it will be sent into Olivia through an i.v."

For the next hour, I swear she doesn't stop talking. I think she is trying to distract me, its working. What could have been an agonizing hour has flown by before I know it.

After she finally told me the story about the frogs, I ran down to the gift shop to buy a giant stuffed frog that I remembered seeing there. When the women saw me dragging it into the room, they all laughed hysterically.

When Fang is finally ready for visitors, I ask her to go with me. As soon as he sees me walking through the door, he gets a big goofy grin on his face. He's obviously still under the influence of anesthesia.

"Beautiful lady!" he shouts. "Come here beautiful lady."

"Shhhh." I giggle. "People are sleeping."

"Wake 'em up then." He says reaching for me.

When I get close enough he grabs my hand, pulling me down into the bed with him.

"Beautiful lady, you're so pretty. Can I keep you?"

I shut him up with a kiss, and whisper, "Forever."

He falls asleep again quickly and I turn back to Mina whom I almost forgot was still in the room.

"I've never seen him so attached to anyone outside the MC before." She grins.

"He didn't mean it. What he said." I shrug looking back at Fang lying in the hospital bed.

"If he said it, then he meant it. I know him."

"Yeah but people say all kinds of crazy things when waking up after surgery. He won't remember what he said."

Although I keep a pleasant smile on my face, my heart actually hurts a little at knowing he won't remember.

"Maybe you're right. I doubt it though. I should go let everyone know that he's doing fine. Do you need a ride to the cabin?" She asks and I'm surprised that she knows that I've been staying there.

"No. Thank you. I'm going to stay for a while."

I smile back at her as she leaves. Looking back at Fang, I move close to the bed leaning down to kiss his brow. His lips tilt up in a small grin while still asleep.

As I leave the room, I look back one last time.

A man as sexy as he is would never want to take on a single mom for the rest of his life. It's rare for a man to want to take on another man's child, especially one as sick as Livie.

Yes she can go into remission but there's no guarantee that she will remain in remission.

Fang

I wake up slowly, squinting at the sun shining through the window of my hospital room.

Rolling to my back, a sharp pain cuts through my side from where they took the bone marrow from my hip. It doesn't hurt as bad as I thought it would though.

I'm catching my breath as though I've been running when my door opens and my Prez walks in with his wife, Mina.

"Ah, you're awake. Good. Thought maybe they gave you too much anesthesia or something." He chuckles.

"Leave him alone! He's just now waking up. Give him at least an hour before you start teasing him." Mina rolls her eyes. "How are you feeling?"

"Pretty good I guess." My voice comes out scratchy and Mina moves to get me a glass of water that I drink down pretty quickly.

"What about Livie? She doing okay?" I ask, handing Mina the cup back.

"She's doing just fine. Autumn said she woke up about an hour ago asking for a hamburger."

I smile at Olivia's antics. She's such a smart little girl.

Looking around my room, I notice a huge stuffed frog sitting in a chair in the corner of the room. A small flash of memory crosses my mind.

"You were in here last night. With Autumn. I remember seeing that stupid frog." I laugh. "You all tell her about that?" I raise my brow.

"Maybe." Mina laughs. "You boys visit for a bit. I'm going to find Autumn and tell her you're awake."

Another memory flashes in my head. One of me asking Autumn if I could keep her. I can't stop my grin that takes over my face.

"Why are you grinning like a loon?" Prez asks with a huff. "What have you done this time?"

"Why do all of you automatically think I've done something wrong?" I demand.

"Because you usually have. You're like the little brother that is always in trouble." Blade says from the door.

Walking in behind him is also Blood and Bear. Two of my other MC brothers.

"What? No gifts for the invalid?" I ask seriously.

"You're invalid alright but it's all in your head." Blood growls back.

"Are all of you harassing the patient?" Dr. Ortez asks, walking into the room.

"He'll survive. For now." Blade laughs.

"Well, he can go home today but he needs to take it easy for at least a week so no crazy pranks for now please." All the guys chuckle at that.

"I'll get Mina to set it up with all the girls to take turns keeping an eye on him." Prez says.

"There's no need. I'll be at the cabin too. Just need someone there with him when I'm here at the hospital with Livie." Autumn says from the door.

I smile in her direction. She's so damn beautiful. She's even more beautiful to me today since she told me last night that I could keep her and Livie forever.

Chapter 5
Fang

I was released from the hospital five days ago. Autumn is here at the cabin with me at night and during the day some of the other girls are here.

I'm mending just fine though, getting around on my own and taking care of most of myself. Everyone else is just being too fussy.

I've been in a hell of a mood that seems to get worse as the days go by mainly because how Autumn has been acting has me wondering if I imagined her saying she would always be mine.

She's kept me at arms length this past week and I do not like it one fucking bit.

Does she really think she can get rid of me so easily?

Slamming my cup down hard on the counter, I take a deep calming breath.

"You okay man?" Dane asks from the doorway.

"I didn't hear you come up." I turn to look at my friend.

He's been extremely quiet lately and I wonder if he's also having an issue with a woman.

"Just thought I'd come check on you. See if you needed anything. It's gotta be hell being stuck here day in and day out." He says as we walk out to the porch.

"It fucking sucks ass! I tried to sneak out yesterday but Mina caught me." I growl, annoyed.

"We heard about that." He chuckles, probably having been told that Mina threatened to actually use a switch on my ass.

"These women are annoying as fuck!" I say loudly hoping they can hear me at the clubhouse.

Dane laughs, shaking his head at me.

"Stop being a puss!" He finally says. "They just want you to get better. No idea why though other than to maybe play another trick on your ass."

"They better not even fucking think about it!"

"Those women? Not thinking? You are asking too much. They are always thinking." He says.

"Fuck! I know and that is scary as hell." I answer and he agrees.

My mind drifts back to Autumn. Could it be that she is thinking too hard about our relationship and getting it all wrong in her head?

"Hey man, you okay? You drifted on me." Dane says, getting my attention.

"Just thinking." I answer.

"Oh shit, did it hurt?" He grins.

"Fuck you, smart ass." I flip him off as he laughs.

Changing the subject, I ask, "So what's been up with you lately?"

"I've been thinking about going Nomad for a while."

His words catch me by surprise.

"What the fuck man? You need to take time to really think about that."

"I have thought about it. A lot actually."

"Does the Prez know?"

"I talked to him about it several weeks ago."

"You're like my closest brother. How could you not tell me before now?" I growl at him, getting pissed off.

"You had other stuff on your mind besides; you'd have tried to talk me out of it."

"I'm still going to try to talk you out of it." I pause waiting for him to say more but he just looks off towards the mountains in the distance.

"This have anything to do with your family?" I finally ask and the look on his face tells me that I'm pretty close to the mark.

"Come on man. Tell me what's going on." I try once again.

"My mom contacted me about a month ago. She said that my dad died and that I should come as soon as I can." He rubs his temples.

Now I understand what is wrong. When Dane left home all those years ago his father basically disowned him for refusing what his family name could give to him.

There was a woman at the time that he thought he was in love with and they were even engaged to be married. He called it off after finding her in bed with his best friend at the time.

The best friend being the same man that Dane's father put in charge of the company business when Dane left home.

"So why do they want you coming back now?" I ask.

"Apparently he never changed his Will." His eyes cut over to me and I can't help the small chuckle that escapes.

"Bet that pisses everyone off."

"I'm going to go and sign everything over to Chris and be done with it."

"Fuck that!" I sit up.

"I don't want it!" He shrugs.

"Don't rush into it. Hell, that stupid fucker may not even be what is right for the company. It's obvious your father thought the same or he would have changed his Will himself."

"I've not thought about it like that." He answers.

"Go and figure it all out first. Look over the books. Just don't rush into signing over what actually belongs to you just because of what happened in the past."

"You sound like Prez." He chuckles.

"Shit, don't tell him that. I'd hate for them to think I'm turning into an adult."

"They'd never believe it anyway." He says and I flip him off again.

Autumn

Pulling up to the cabin, I grab the large envelope from the passenger side seat.

I'm not sure what's inside of it. Livie made me swear that I wouldn't peek at whatever gift she made for Fang.

My heart skips a beat at how close she is to him. They still talk every single night before she goes to sleep.

I've tried to get her to tell me what they talk about but according to her it's all top secret stuff.

Walking towards the cabin, I'm surprised to not see Fang waiting for me at the door which has become his habit.

As I walk inside, the smell of something delicious hits my senses and my stomach growls reminding me that I didn't eat much today.

"Hey ya. Are you hungry?" Fang's smiling face pops out from the kitchen and I head his way.

"What are you cooking?" I ask, walking into the kitchen as Fang stirs something on the stove.

"My super famous chili." He grins back at me.

I chuckle at his expression. "Super famous, huh? If it's famous, why is this the first time I'm hearing about it?"

"Because the recipe is top secret of course."

"I think there are only a few ways to make chili and they all basically taste the same."

He spins around, looking at me with a wide eyed expression and a mock gasp.

"You wound me!" He throws his hand over his heart and I can't stop myself from laughing at him.

"You are a nut!"

Raising his brow at me, he says, "You'd like to see my what?"

My face immediately burns and I know it's turning red. With a grin I ask, "Are you ever serious?"

His eyes hold mine as he turns off the stove and walks closer to me, backing me against the counter.

"Only when I have to be. Besides, I like watching your cheeks turn all red. Makes me wonder if the rest of you turns that color." He whispers and I shiver from his closeness.

We've not been intimate together since before the surgery.

At night, when I close my eyes, I can still feel his skin against my own.

"I've missed you Autumn." He leans closer until his nose is close to my ear, kissing me softly just below.

My entire body feels electrified and I lean in closer to him needing to feel his heat against me. My hands come up to grab him.

Having forgotten the envelope in my hand, it falls to the floor.

Pulling back away from me, Fang looks down at it.

"What's this?" He asks, bending down to pick it up.

My thoughts are still scattered so I shake my head lightly to clear it.

"Um, Livie sent it to you. I wasn't allowed to open it." I shrug but Fang grins widely as he moves to open it.

He pulls out a piece of paper and I see his eyes as they light up from whatever is on it.

Confused, I ask, "What is it?"

"The most beautiful picture in the world." He whispers, turning to the refrigerator and using the magnets there to hold it up.

Walking over so that I can see it, I notice that she has drawn a picture of all three of us holding hands in a field of flowers.

At the top, in her little girl handwriting are three simple words.

My heart races as I look at them, afraid of what I have no idea.

A man scared of a little girl getting attached to him wouldn't have looked the way Fang did when he pulled this drawing out of an envelope.

That look was one of a man who sees himself next to her but at what kind of capacity?

A friend?

A long distance one?

Will he still keep in touch once we leave?

"She loves you." I say, looking over at him and just now noticing that he's setting the table.

"Good because I love her too." He grins.

"No. I mean she actually loves you Fang."

Drawing his brows together he looks at me. "Is something wrong, Autumn? Because I'm not following." He crosses his arms over his broad chest.

"She's attached to you. You can't just disappear from her life."

He looks back at me for several long minutes before one brow rises as if to ask me if there's more.

"Why the fuck would you think I would disappear from her life exactly?"

His voice is more serious than I've ever heard it to be.

"You'll get tired of us eventually and want to get back to your life. Besides, we can't stay here in your space forever."

I stare back at him for several long minutes until his face changes and he starts laughing.

"What the hell is so funny?" I demand, my hands moving to my hips.

He comes at me quickly, once again backing me into the counter but this time he cages me in with his arms.

Leaning in until he's only an inch from my face and he's all I can see.

"I do believe a certain someone told me that I could keep the two of you for the rest of my life. Is that not what you told me, Autumn?"

I'm breathing rapidly but with each breath his cologne sweeps up my nose and he's all I can smell.

A smell that seems to be a drug to me as all I want to do is reach out and taste him.

"Answer me. Is that not what you told me?"

"Yes." I finally whisper.

"You taking that promise back?" His hand comes up to cup my cheek.

"Not if you actually want us."

I finally answer and his playful grin spreads slowly across his face once again.

"Olivia is going to be my best friend for the rest of my life. So yeah, I want her in my life forever. As for you, let me show you just how much I want you." He whispers before his mouth takes mine in a fevered long overdue kiss that has me soaking and ready to beg if need be.

My arms come up to pull him closer. His hardness pushes into my stomach and I try to lift myself up so that I can feel him where I need him most right now.

His hands reach down grabbing my thighs, lifting me up and I wrap my legs around him.

I feel us moving but I don't open my eyes or remove my mouth from his. He kicks a door open before breaking our kiss.

Sliding me down the front of his body, his hands grab my sweater jerking it over my head.

Pushing the straps of my bra off my shoulders, my breasts spring free for only a second before his mouth is on me, sucking hard.

He lets go when I feel him laying me back on the bed. I open my eyes and watch him as he pulls all of his clothes off quickly before ridding me of the rest of mine.

I giggle at his rush for us both to be naked.

Crawling over me, he presses his heat to my own.

"I told you I missed you." He whispers, kissing me deeply again as he grinds us together, soaking himself in my wetness.

"I missed you too." I whisper back when he pulls away from the kiss.

His hips pull back slightly and I feel his cock line up with my now throbbing center. Holding my eyes with his, he slips inside in one fluid stroke.

My eyes roll back in my head from the pleasure of being filled. He growls slightly when my insides squeeze his cock in a rhythm that demands he moves.

"Fuck baby. You keep doing that; I'm not going to last long." He growls.

"Then fuck me so we both don't last long." I groan, lifting my hips to grind on him.

He pulls back, slamming into me quickly. My hands move to my breasts on their own, cupping them. His mouth comes down, taking my left nipple in, biting just hard enough to send pleasure to my core.

He picks up speed, slamming into me hard each time. The pull of his mouth on my breast along with the fullness of him, I'm climbing higher and higher.

The second one of his hands moves to my clit, pinching it, I explode on his cock with a scream and he follows with his own right behind me.

"Damn this man is too perfect." Is the last thought I have before I fall deeply asleep.

Chapter 6
Autumn

It's been almost two months since Olivia's transplant and she's getting more stir crazy each day. Not that I can blame her.

She's a kid that should be able to go outside and play in the snow.

Instead she's stuck inside a sterilized room inside the hospital.

"How much longer?" She whines, looking at Dr. Ortez.

"It's hard to say exactly. We have to wait and make sure that your body is reacting as it should and taking to the new marrow well." He explains but she rolls her eyes, turning to look out the window with a huff.

"The nurses will be around in the morning to draw some blood, check all of her levels and I'll have a better idea of where we are." He says.

"Thank you, Dr. Ortez. For everything." I smile although he can't see it because of the surgical mask on my face.

"Wait to thank me once we know how this ends." He answers, walking out.

Having watched the doctor since we've been here, I've come to learn that he has a hard time accepting thanks, especially when he doesn't yet know if what he has done will be a success.

"Where's Fang?" Livie asks, drawing my attention.

"He's at work today but said to tell you that he'd be popping in to check on you tomorrow."

"He promised to take me to see the horses once I get out of here." She announces with bright eyes.

I now understand her pushing so hard about when she'll get released.

"You can't push yourself to get out of here quicker than your body will allow you know. It takes whatever time it takes."

A nurse comes in with a tray for Olivia. It smells really good and my stomach grumbles.

Looking down at my watch to check the time, I see that I have enough time to swing by Bella's place to pick something up for dinner before meeting Fang at the cabin.

"I'm going to go and I'll be back first thing in the morning."

"Okay mom. Tell Fang I'll call before bed."

I smile, having already known what she was going to say.

Every evening is always the same between those two. I still have no idea what all they talk about.

Blowing her a mock kiss since I'm not allowed to actually touch her, I turn to the door and walk out.

I take the paper scrubs, gloves and mask off once I am outside of her room, throwing them in the bin.

Several nurses and aids pass me in the hall, calling out a good night as I make my way to the front door.

Once outside, I pull my jacket closed from the snowy wind.

I'm just getting to the jeep when I hear someone behind me.

Turning around, I gasp just as they grab my arm, squeezing hard.

My eyes collide with the face in front of me. A face that I had hoped to never see again.

"Hello Autumn."

"What are you doing here, Leo?" I ask, trying not to show much of a reaction.

"It's been a while. Thought I'd come check in, see about our little girl."

He smiles but it doesn't reach his eyes. Eyes that seem to be scanning the area the same way he used to do when someone was looking for him.

"Our little girl?" I raise a brow at him. "Since when do you even care?" I demand.

His eyes go hard just as his hand on my arm squeezes a little harder until I wince.

"Just tell me what you want, Leo. Stop pretending." I growl through clenched teeth.

His lip curls but suddenly his face changes with a grin, confirming what I already know.

That he's here for a reason and that reason is not our daughter.

"I heard about all that donation money you got back in Alaska."

My eyes narrow but I wait, saying nothing.

"I want half of it. I know you got like one hundred thousand or some shit. I want my half."

"Your half? That money doesn't belong to you!" I try to jerk away from him but he holds tightly, getting close to my face.

"That fucking brat you were hell bent on keeping is half mine therefore any money you get for her is half mine!"

"It was donations for a specific cause. I don't get access to that!"

"You're fucking lying and I know it!" He shoves me against the wall, pinning me there with his body and holding my arms down.

My heart beats quickly and I feel as though I can't catch my breath.

"Hmm, someone sure has filled out nicely." He whispers, pushing himself further into me.

Within seconds, I can feel him getting hard behind his zipper.

My stomach rolls and I know if I had anything in it, I would throw up all over him.

"Let me go!" I demand.

He grabs my face with his hand, digging his fingers in and I know there will be bruises.

"You have one fucking week to get me my money or else Autumn. You hear me?"

"Or else what, Leo?" I ask, wondering what he actually could do to me at this point.

He grabs both my arms so fast that I don't have time to react, stretching them both above my head.

My shirt pulls up, exposing my skin to the cold air.

Holding my hands up with only one of his, he moves his other hand down to my waist and I start to shake when I feel his hand on my bare skin.

Looking me straight in the eye, he pushes my shirt up grabbing my breast in his hand, rubbing it lightly.

"You really want to find out Autumn?" He grins at my wide scared eyes.

Squeezing my breast hard one last time, he shoves away from me.

"One fucking week." He growls, turning and disappearing into the night.

Once I can no longer see him, I gasp in the air like I had stopped breathing and that is when the tears begin to fall.

Shaking hard, I open the jeep door and climb in, starting it up quickly.

I spin tires out of the parking lot as I head down the road.

My only thought is to get to Bella's Brew where I know I'll be safe.

Fang

"Man, you smell like shit!" Wrench laughs while holding his nose.

"Laugh away jackass, it'll be your turn to haul the manure again next week." Blood growls before downing the rest of his beer.

"Yeah but I don't smell that bad after. What the fuck did you do? Lay down and take a nap in it?"

"Actually, his horse pushed him." Prez laughs.

"When the fuck did we become ranch hands anyway? Thought we were only helping out until Hayden could hire her own men. We've been doing most of the work for a couple years now." Blood asks.

"I've actually been going through the applications that she has picked from those that have applied to the ad. Soon you can go back to only working on bikes." Prez announces.

Getting real ranch hands for Wolf's Landing will free most of us up for more custom work on bikes as well as cars.

It's what we are good at and what we love.

Plus, a bike or car isn't likely to shove us into a pile of manure.

"How's the kid doing?" Blade asks from beside me.

"Going crazy from having to stay in that room from what I can tell. She told me last night on the phone she knew the best time to just walk out without anyone knowing because she knows all the nurses routines." I shake my head as he laughs.

"Sounds like a smart girl to me."

"I'd say she's a smartass most days." I grin.

"You sure she isn't yours then?" The Prez pipes up, making all the guys laugh.

"I'm sure but I sure wouldn't mind if she was mine though."

"It's like that?" Prez asks.

"It's definitely like that." I answer seriously.

"Good for you, man." Blade slaps my back.

"Anyone want another?" Dane asks, walking behind the counter at the bar of the clubhouse.

My phone starts buzzing in my pocket.

Taking it out, I see that it's Bella and my brows draw together wondering why she would be calling me.

Stepping away from the guys, I push to answer it.

"Bella? Everything okay?" I ask, looking back at the guys and seeing that I now had their attention as well, especially my VP, Blade.

"You need to get over here. Autumn is here and looks scared to death. She was crying when she got here. I thought she was going to run your jeep into the front of the cafe from the way she was driving." Bella says quickly.

"Is it Livie?" My heart races.

"She hasn't said much of anything. She's stopped crying but is now mostly looking out the windows."

"I'll be there in a few minutes. Make sure she doesn't leave." I instruct, turning the phone off quickly.

"What's up?" Blade asks, coming closer.

"It's Autumn. Bella says she showed up crying and she can't get any answers from her about what's wrong."

"Need us to come with you?" He looks concerned as well.

That's what I love about the MC family.

We are always there for each other, thicker than any blood family ever could be.

"Nah, man. It might be something to do with Livie and she may not want everyone to know just yet."

My heart beats even faster at the thought of anything happening to that little girl I've come to love more than my own life.

"Let us know as soon as you know something." Prez says, nodding my way and I nod back, turning to the door.

The entire way there I try not to let my imagination get the best of me of what could be wrong.

Worrying over something that you have no control over does absolutely no fucking good anyway.

I see Autumn through the window as I pull my own jeep up next to the one I've been letting my girl use.

Jumping out quickly, not bothering to turn the jeep off, I rush inside the door to Bella's Brew.

Bella sees me coming and moves away from the table as I slide in next to Autumn.

She jumps when I lay my hand on her arm.

"It's just me." I whisper.

Tears quickly cloud her eyes and I pull her even closer to me.

"What is Autumn? What's happened? Is it Livie?" I ask.

Her head shakes and the tightness inside my chest eases for only a moment.

"Did someone hurt you?" I ask through clenched teeth.

She goes way too still in my arms without answering me.

All the muscles in my body tighten wondering who in this fucking town would dare touch someone protected by the MC.

"I need you to tell me what happened baby." I whisper.

Pulling back from me, she looks me in the eyes with the saddest look I've ever seen.

"I just want to go home. Can we go home?" She asks in a small voice and my heart breaks.

"We'll go in my jeep. It should be nice and warm there now. Give me your keys. I'll get one of the guys to drop yours off later."

I hold my hand out to her until she places them in my palm. As I move to get up, her hand tightens on my jacket.

"I'll be right back. I'm going to get Bella to give your keys to Blade." I explain and wait until she lets go.

She looks so small sitting there in that booth. Not at all like the woman I've come to love.

"Is she okay?" Bella asks as I get to the counter.

"I'm not exactly sure yet. Can you give her keys to Blade? He'll get someone to drop it off at the cabin later."

"Sure." She takes the keys, putting them in her pocket.

"Did she say anything at all before I got here?" I ask quietly.

"No. Well, I think I heard her say that He's Back. But when I asked her what she said, she didn't repeat it." Bella shrugs.

"Thanks Bella."

"Not a problem Fang. You are family." She smiles.

Turning around, I head over to the table to get my girl to take her home. I'll let her rest for a while but at some point she will be telling me everything that happened.

I don't take too kindly to anyone hurting what's mine. Autumn and Olivia are definitely mine.

I don't give a fuck how that makes me sound. I love those two. I'll not let anyone hurt them and get away with it.

They'll pay for it with their life.

Chapter 7
Fang

As soon as we got home last night, I made Autumn eat something before we lay on the bed together and she quickly fell asleep.

I know she'll be getting up soon so I'm fixing breakfast and hopefully she can tell me exactly what happened last night.

When I undressed her for bed, I noticed hand prints on her arms from where someone had grabbed her.

It took everything in me not to roar out my anger at seeing bruises on my woman.

I'm just putting our plates on the table when I hear her walk into the room behind me.

"Morning, beautiful. Hungry?" I turn with a smile.

"Thank you." She gives me a small smile back and the tension inside me lessens knowing that she may be more open today to letting me in.

"Have a seat. I'll get us some orange juice."

Grabbing the juice, I pour our glasses before taking the seat next to her.

"Mmm, I love bacon." She groans, taking a slice and putting it in her mouth.

I chuckle at the look of pure joy that comes over her face at that first bite.

"Jesus, woman."

"What?" She asks around a mouth full.

"Don't think I've ever seen anyone enjoy bacon that much."

"It's so good. Livie and I couldn't afford much bacon back home. We had it so rarely." She gets this far off look on her face.

It hurts me to think about the struggles those two possibly faced before coming here.

Come to think about it, she's never really told me much about her life before.

"Ready to talk about last night?" I ask, watching as she turns to me with a look of sadness.

Reaching over, I put her hand inside my own.

"I really do need you to tell me who left those bruises on your arms." I hold her eyes with my own.

"I've really never told you anything about Olivia's dad." She begins and my brows draw together.

"He have something to do with those?" I nod to the bruises.

"Yes."

My entire body tenses up again and I wonder why she has acted as though he wasn't around.

"I thought he wasn't in your life anymore." I state.

"He's not. Not really. He left us both a long time ago but he has this habit of finding us and bringing trouble with him."

"What kind of trouble?" I ask.

"The kind that has mean looking men knocking down your door at midnight and holding a gun to your head, demanding to know where he is because he told them he lived there." She sighs, rubbing her temples.

"He into drugs?" I ask.

"Drugs, gambling, you name it and he's right in the middle."

"So why is he here now?"

"He heard about the donations that were collected for Olivia back home. Someone told him that I got over a hundred thousand dollars and he wants his share." She laughs sarcastically. "Claims it's half his because Olivia is his child." She rolls her eyes.

I feel a tick in my jaw as my anger boils under the surface.

"He must owe someone and wants the money to pay them."

"But I don't have the money to give him. The church handled the donations and paid it all directly to the hospital."

"Even if you had it, I wouldn't let you give it to him. As you've already said, he'll just keep coming back. Now tell me how he put those bruises on you." I narrow my eyes.

"He pinned me against the side of the jeep." Her eyes look everywhere but at me and I know she's not telling me all of it.

"He put his hands anywhere else?" I ask softly, leaning closer and turning her face to look directly at me.

Her eyes cloud up with tears and my teeth grind together with the rage threatening to explode inside of me.

Leaning all the way in, I take her sweet mouth with my own until she fully kisses me back.

Breaking off the kiss, I give her a small smile.

"It'll be okay. I promise that I will not let anyone hurt you again. Neither of you."

Autumn

"Fang said you were already asleep when I called last night." Livie says from her side of the checkers board.

"I was really tired sweetheart."

I look at her with a soft smile, hoping that she doesn't see through my lie.

There's no point in me telling her about her father. It'll only make her agitated and possibly scared.

She learned a long time ago that he couldn't be trusted.

Something no child should ever have to learn about one of their parents.

I only want her concentrating on getting better. She and her health are the most important things in my life.

I just hope there's a day where we can breathe easy without worrying about her getting sicker or worse.

"I can't wait for it to warm up outside." Livie says drawing my attention back to her.

I chuckle slightly as she sighs.

"Why is that?" I ask.

"I'll be out of this hospital for one thing." She huffs, rolling her eyes. "Plus Fang says that the club has weekly cookouts for the whole family."

"The whole family?" My brows draw together.

"Yeah. He says that everyone in the club is family even though they're not really from the same family. You know. Like me and you. We are the same family."

"Yes we are." I smile at her.

"The club is a family they all created and take care of each other. Like a family is supposed to do."

I shake my head listening to every word. She apparently has much deeper conversations with Fang than I do. I've never taken the time to really ask him about the club.

"Like I take care of you." I grin, wanting so badly to put my arms around her but that still isn't allowed.

The nurse told me this morning though that we may be almost through the worst part of everything. She said the doctor would be around to confirm test results.

My sweet baby girl could be coming home soon.

"We'll be able to go home soon. Back to Alaska." As soon as the words leave my mouth, Olivia sets her face into stone.

"This is home!"

"This isn't our home sweetheart." I start to explain but she jumps up from the bed stomping her way over to the window.

"Fang is our family. The motorcycle club is our family. I will not leave!" She stomps her little foot one last time for good measure.

The doctor knocks on the door, getting my attention and I turn in that direction.

Looking back at Livie, I say, "We still have plenty of time to talk about this. Okay?"

"We ain't talking because I ain't leaving!"

She raises her own brows and I do my best to not smile at the fact she looks exactly the same way I do when I set my mind to something.

Instead I turn towards the door to see what the doctor needs.

"I'll be right back sweetie." I tell her but she doesn't say anything back.

It's her way of letting me know that she is mad and dead set on staying.

I find the doctor once I'm in the hall and walk over to him.

"Is something wrong?" I ask.

"Not at all." Dr. Ortez says with a smile. "Her weekly test results are showing a huge improvement."

"That's really great." My voice cracks.

"It really is. In a few more weeks she should be okay to move into outpatient care for a while."

"Outpatient? Can she not do that back home in Alaska?" I ask, wondering if I'm going to have to impose on Fang even longer than anticipated.

The thought of having to stay with him longer actually makes me feel more relief than anything.

Looking back up at the doctor he has a look of confusion on his face.

"Does Fang know you are planning to leave?" He asks softly.

"What does that matter?"

My back straightens at anyone thinking that I have to ask permission to do anything.

Besides, I've got to get Olivia out of here and somewhere safe. Somewhere far away from Leo.

Doctor Ortez slowly smiles. "I think you know exactly why I am asking. That man is in love with you and if you think he won't fight to keep you, you're badly mistaken."

"I'm not completely oblivious to what happens in motorcycle clubs. It probably wouldn't take him three whole days to forget me." I chuckle.

Leaning in closer to me, he says, "I know those men. Hell, I'm basically one of them. When they find that special one, everyone within a hundred mile radius knows. He's picked you as the one to hold his heart forever. Make no mistake; he'll tear himself to pieces to keep the two of you right next to him."

He leaves me standing there with my mouth hanging open, surprised at how forthright he was with me. I'm still lost in thought when I see a face at the end of the hall in a crowd.

Walking fast to the corner, I look down to the other corner but don't see Leo. I know he was there though as every hair on my neck stands on end.

Fang

Looking around the room filled to the brim with my brothers, I'm thankful for every one of these men.

As soon as I called Prez letting him know the situation with Autumn, he called everyone in for Church.

They were all already here by the time I got here after dropping Autumn off at the hospital.

Even Baratta, Blood's brother in law, is here even though he's not a member.

"I thought I had recognized that name so I called my Uncle who had quite a lot to say." Baratta says from beside the door.

"Leo owes quite a chunk of money, mostly to Uncle Tony. His men have been looking for him in Alaska since that seems to be where he usually runs to."

"From what I can find, he seems to jump from one place to the next but has been down in Vegas for the past year." Snake says over the lid of his laptop.

"So gambling debts. How much does he owe?" Prez asks, looking at Baratta.

"Around a hundred grand."

"Fucking hell. Why would they loan a piece of shit like him that much?" I demand to know.

"Because for a while, he was on a winning streak." Baratta shrugs and I look at him hard. "Look, you know as well as I do how this shit works."

"He's right. It's not his Uncle's fault. That blame rests solely on that asshole's shoulders."

Shaking my head in agreement because I know that he's right, I ask instead, "So what's the plan?"

Prez looks to Blade, our VP, "I want two men inside the hospital on the floor where Olivia is staying.

I also want two stationed outside in the parking lot watching the doors. Rotate them out every twelve hours.

In the meantime, I want everyone looking for where this fool is staying."

Blade nods his agreement that it'll be done.

Looking at the rest of the men, he says, "I don't want Olivia or Autumn left anywhere at any time without someone with them. This fucker felt safe to physically assault one of our own. I'd say it's time we paid that kindness back."

He grins as the rest of us bang our fists on the table.

I watch as all my brothers file out of the room and I hang back to speak to the Prez.

"So have you told her yet?" Prez asks as soon as the last man is out of the room.

"Told her what?" I ask, confused.

"That you are claiming her."

"She already knows that I claim her." My brows draw together.

"You sure about that?"

When I continue to look at him with nothing to say, he continues, "She was just asking Dr. Ortez earlier today about how soon after Olivia is released that they could go home. To Alaska."

"Like hell!" I step forward and Prez holds his hand up to stop me.

"As I said. You need to explain to her about your claim. And put a ring on it. That would probably help keep her in one spot."

He chuckles at my wild eyed look.

After a few long seconds of thinking about it, I begin to grin.

"Think of something, did you?" He asks, still laughing at me.

"You damn straight I did. Thanks Prez!" I slap him on the back as I rush out of the room.

He's right. I've never made it completely clear to her about us. The last time we talked about it was when we fucked each others brains out.

I know from being around all the other ole ladies that they need the words at random times.

Out of the blue otherwise they'll think it's just a way for us to get in their pants.

I'll remedy that thinking as soon as possible. There will never be any more doubts in her mind once I'm done either.

Chapter 8
Autumn

It feels as though I'm going crazy. I see Leo's face almost everywhere I go but when the guys go check, he's not there.

Fang asked me if it were possible that I was just so scared that my mind was playing tricks on me.

It's possible I guess but I really don't think that is the reason.

I know Leo. He's a sneaky bastard that will bide his time before exacting his plan.

Whatever his plan is this time.

The last time when he found us, I slipped up by not checking to be sure that our doors were locked.

It was the only time I ever slipped up and it cost us greatly.

He stole every bit of money I had saved in a coffee can and left me with a swollen face. Livie watched it all from her hiding spot under my bed.

Of course I went to the cops, just as I always did but they can't protect us.

A restraining order is just a piece of paper. Worth nothing.

He left town again before they could find him. I always knew he'd be back again, I just didn't know when.

I probably should have moved again, made it a little harder but what was the point when he has found us every single time.

"Mom! It's your turn." Olivia pulls me from my thoughts.

"Sorry kiddo." I smile, moving my checker piece.

"I'm really tired of checkers." She groans.

"Hmm, I can see what else I can find at the store before coming here in the morning if you want me to."

"Find something fun! Like one of those handheld games that makes all the noise." She smiles brightly.

Hearing the door open behind us, we both smile at the man walking in.

"Hey, Munchkin!" Fang greets Livie.

"You didn't tell me you were coming today!" Livie says excitedly.

Pulling a package from behind his back, he answers, "Well you did say you were so tired of checkers and you hated trying to play it by yourself. So I brought you something."

I look at him with a question on my face but he's too busy watching Olivia tear into the paper.

She pulls out one of the games she was just asking me for while jumping up and down in place.

"Oh my God! Thank you so much Fang!" She smiles more brightly than I've seen her do in a really long time.

"You're welcome, Munchkin." He grins.

"Okay. Smoker man!" She rolls her eyes.

"Hey! You can't call me that! I quit smoking, remember?"

"You still used to do it so the name still fits." She sticks her tongue out at him.

Grabbing his chest where his heart is, he says, "You wound me."

She looks over at him carefully before saying, "Nah, you ain't bleeding."

They both break out into laughter and watch as the two of them open up her new game, setting it up for her to play.

He's so good with her and I can tell they both are attached to each other.

Looking at Fang, I'd say I'm pretty attached myself.

For the next hour I watch them take turns playing the game before it's time for us to go for the night.

The doctor has finally started allowing us to hug her before we go and I take several long minutes to hold her to me.

"You're gonna smother me." She mumbles into my chest.

"Sorry." I pull back from her. "I've just missed being able to do that."

She smiles brightly at me before walking over to hug Fang just as tight.

"Goodnight sweetheart." I say from the door.

"Night Munchkin!"

"Night Smoker Man!"

She giggles as the door closes behind us.

"God, I love that kid!" Fang says from beside me as we walk down the hall.

"I'm glad that you do." I say honestly, looking up into his face.

He stops walking, pulling me to him.

"She's not the only one I have feelings for, you know." He holds my eyes.

My heart speeds up but I'm not sure what I should say.

Instead, he kisses me softly before taking my hand and walking us both out the door.

Fang

Lying here watching her sleep has become one of my favorite pastimes.

She's so beautiful to me no matter what but in these quiet times, when she's completely relaxed in my arms, she's even more beautiful to me.

She didn't say anything back to me at the hospital when I hinted at the feelings I have for her. That didn't bother me though.

She'll know soon enough just how much I mean those three little words before I say them out loud.

I'm a man with a plan and part of that plan is to ask Olivia everything first as she is just as important to me as her mother is.

I smile to myself thinking about our short phone call earlier.

It was the shortest one we've ever had because she was so into that new game that I gave her earlier tonight.

I don't think I've ever seen anyone's eyes light up as bright as her's did when she opened that package.

It gave me the most wonderful feeling knowing that I could do that for her.

She's one of the coolest little kids I've ever been around. Her sense of humor matches my own.

I couldn't have made a little girl more like me if I had created her myself.

Looking over at the clock, I slip back out of bed, grabbing my phone and head towards the kitchen, wanting to check in with the Prez.

"What's up man?" He answers almost on the first ring.

"Anything new?"

"Not really. We've had people around town who said they've spotted him but they don't know where he's staying. It can't be that far from here considering that he's spotted daily."

"Autumn keeps swearing she sees him everywhere. I think it's bothering her more than she's letting on." I look back down the hall where she's sleeping.

"We'll find him. We always find them. I will say he's one sneaky bastard." Prez growls through the phone.

"Yeah, he is. Change of subject, I may need some of the guys' help next week if we can spare anyone."

"What for?" He questions.

"I want to finish up that back bedroom here at the cabin. Fix it up for Livie."

"So you've had that discussion with Autumn like you and I talked about finally?"

"Not yet actually but I'm working on it." I chuckle.

"Oh, you plan to get that sweet little girl to help you rope in the mom." He laughs.

"I'm fairly certain that sweet little girl is already on my side." I smile.

"I'm happy for you man. You deserve it. I can't wait to get to know Livie more once she's out of the hospital. Doc says she's pretty outspoken and a complete jokester."

"Yep. Just think of all the jokes I can get her to help me out with."

"Shit, one of you is more than enough. Don't know if this Club can handle another one that acts just like you."

"We're about to find out." I grin broadly as we get off the phone.

I can't wait to make our little family official. I'll be a dad.

Oh fuck! I'll be a dad to a little girl!

Olivia

Walking over to the table close to the window, I plug my new game up so that it'll charge.

As I start to turn away, I see someone out in the parking lot leaning against the hood of a car.

The man looks to be looking up directly at my window and I get a weird feeling about it.

I can't make out much of his features but he seems familiar somehow but I don't know why.

Turning away from the window, I go back to my bed and pull the covers up to my neck.

I can tell that the transplant as well as the medicine has been working as I feel so much stronger than I did when I was so sick.

Who could have guessed that I would find my miracle on a cold day from a man named Fang.

I giggle still at his name.

It really is quite funny to call someone that.

Fang says that most of the guys in the motorcycle club have what's known as club names.

All of them are weird but somehow fit each man.

I can't wait to meet them.

I've seen the way my mom looks at him and I've seen how he looks at her.

I pray every single night that they will fall in love and that I'll finally have a dad.

I know that he wouldn't be the dad I was born with and good thing too.

That man was awful mean.

He's not been around again since that last time when he hurt my mom.

For a long time after that, I couldn't sleep very long without jumping awake afraid that he was there again.

I swore that I'd never let him hurt her that way again. I'd kill him myself if I had to.

I don't care how little I am. I'd find a way to do it.

Saying my prayers quietly into my pillow, I close my eyes and sleep the rest of the night, forgetting about the man in the parking lot below.

Chapter 9
Fang

Carrying the two small packages in my hand, I nod to the prospects sitting at the other end of the hall as I open the door to Olivia's hospital room.

"Fang!" She exclaims excitedly and Autumn's eyes jump to mine in surprise.

I didn't tell either of them that I was coming today. It's all part of the surprise I've planned out to get them both on board with moving in with me.

It's only a small part of my plan.

I have every intention of eventually claiming Autumn as my wife, making Olivia my daughter in every way that counts is a bonus.

"What are you doing here?" Autumn asks with a smile.

"I wanted to see my two favorite girls and ask them something." I grin widely.

"Do you have me another present?"

Livie demands with her hands on her hips as she eyes the two small boxes in my hand.

"Um, sort of."

I chuckle as she bounces up and down excitedly.

I've figured out that I could give this sweet little girl a rock and she'd be overjoyed with excitement.

That's part of what makes her so special. She reminds me of my little brother so much.

He was exactly like her.

I gave him a marble that I found in a parking lot one time and his eyes lit up with the purest joy.

"There's two." She points to the presents. "Are they both for me?" Livie asks.

"One is actually for your mom." My eyes look over at Autumn who looks at me oddly.

"Well, gimme!" She holds her little hands out.

Handing her the one with her name on it, I sit on the edge of her bed and watch as she carefully opens it.

She pulls out a key that I had specially made for her with the Wolfsbane Logo etched into one side and her name on the other attached to a chain so she can keep it around her neck.

"This is so pretty! But what does it go to?" She asks.

"To your new bedroom at my cabin. Or our cabin. At least I'm hoping for it to be our cabin. You, me and your mom." I look between the two.

Autumn looks stunned while Olivia's eyes begin to tear up.

"Hey. I didn't mean to make you cry. Do you not want to stay with me?"

I ask as a small pain enters my heart at the thought she may not want to stick around after she is released from the hospital.

Her big eyes stare back at me before she jumps into my arms, crying into my shoulder.

"I want very much to stay." She mumbles into my shirt without looking up.

Looking over the top of her head at Autumn, I see that she's trying to not cry now as well.

Still holding Livie close to me, I hold out the last package to Autumn.

"Your turn." I say simply.

She takes her time opening the package which has the same kind of key inside that I had made for Livie.

I've not mentioned to them the other function for this type of key.

There's a very tiny microchip inside that gives off a signal that Snake can track from any computer.

We learned years ago to start making sure we had a way to track those that we love in case of anything happening.

"Will you both move in with me?" I ask Autumn who still has said anything.

Her eyes look back at me for several long minutes and I start to wonder if she'll remain silent on the subject.

"I don't know what to say." She whispers, looking back down at the key in her hand. "I need time to think about it."

"You've got time. I'll never rush you."

I reach out cupping her face with my one free hand and still holding Livie close to me.

These two mean the absolute world to me. I just need them both to start believing it.

Believing in me.

To lose them would completely destroy me.

Autumn

Opening the box, I admire the beautiful key that Fang had made for me.

Olivia is currently wearing hers around her neck and hasn't stopped smiling since she opened it.

"They are really pretty." Livie draws my attention back to her.

"Yes they are."

"I want to stay mom."

"I know you do, baby." I smile, closing the box and sticking it in my jacket pocket.

"Do you not like him?"

Her question catches me by surprise. "Who?"

"Fang. Duh." Her eyes roll.

"You keep rolling those eyes and they're going to get stuck in the back of your head." I warn and she giggles. "Of course I like him." I finally answer her.

"Me too. He's not like Leo." Her face goes hard when she says his name. She stopped calling him dad a really long time ago.

My own heart kicks up at the reminder that he's here. In this town, once again making threats against me.

"He's certainly different from Leo." I agree with her.

"He'd make a good dad." She nods her head firmly as if she has already decided.

She probably has and it would do no one absolutely any good to try to change her mind.

"He didn't ask me to marry him." I say to her but she just grins back at me.

"He's going to and then he'll be my dad."

"What makes you so sure I'll say yes little lady?" I chuckle at her.

"You can't fool me mom." She laughs as we hear the door open behind us.

"I have some amazing news for you today." Dr. Ortez announces with a huge smile.

"I can go home?" Livie jumps up with a huge hopeful grin.

"One more week and if everything is still going as it has been, I'll release you for out patient care." He smiles as she starts jumping around excitedly.

I can't stop the tears escaping my eyes as I am overwhelmed with the news that she is doing so well.

Leo

I move into my little hiding place inside the kitchen of the cafeteria that gives me a clear view of who comes through the doors.

I've watched Autumn for a while now and she always has the same routine.

A few times I purposely let her see me just so I could relish in the fear that spread across her face.

The motorcycle guys have made things a little harder but not impossible.

While they may come into the cafeteria with her, they don't always pay attention.

I once again wonder how the hell she got mixed up with the club.

Doesn't that stupid bitch know what kind of men join clubs such as this?

I've watched her with that one they call Fang.

The way she looks at him, I know she's putting out for him.

She has to be since she goes home with him every night.

I've followed them quite a few times. The first night I had to stop myself from sneaking in and shooting them both.

Instead, I decided to wait for the perfect time and take her right from under his nose.

We used to have a good life back before that brat came along.

She waited until it was too late to tell me she was pregnant.

I hated the idea at first but thought what the hell; the kid would keep her occupied at home while I was gone.

It was when I realized that the kid would take up all her fucking time that I knew it was a mistake to have allowed her to come into the world.

Always at doctors offices and staying weeks on end at hospitals while ignoring me. The one that should have been most important in her life.

I'll get my money but I also plan to remind her just who the fuck she belongs to.

Closing my eyes, I remember our last time together.

It's been too long and I can't wait to feel her once again before I sell her to the highest bidder.

Adjusting myself behind my zipper, I watch the door waiting for what's mine.

Chapter 10
Autumn

Walking into the cafeteria, I turn towards the line for the hot food on the other side of the room while the Wolfsbane prospect goes to find a table.

He always picks a spot where he can watch the doors without his back being turned towards them.

It's a lot more crowded here at this time of day which is why I usually wait until an hour after lunch but the nurses were in Olivia's room for tests so I decided to have my lunch now instead of later.

I'm just grabbing a plate from the side bar when I feel someone come up behind me.

I don't think anything of it until I feel something pressed into my side at the same time I hear Leo's voice.

"Walk slowly towards the exit right behind us." He says quietly.

Not three feet away is an exit that leads directly outside of the hospital.

It's the same one that Olivia used that day when I found her outside talking to Fang for the first time.

Out of the corner of my eye, I can see the Prospect sitting at a table towards the back. His eyes aren't on me though.

Instead he seems to be typing on his phone.

"Move! Now!" Leo demands, poking me hard in the side with what feels like a gun.

Leaving my food where it's at, I turn slowly and walk the few steps to the exit, praying that someone will notice something isn't right before we make it out the door.

I wonder briefly if I should scream. It's possible he could shoot me but we are in a hospital. Surely I wouldn't die from a gunshot here.

I do know that it's possible I could die if I allow him to take me from here though.

"Don't even think about it." He says through clenched teeth.

Once outside the doors, he grabs me by the arm and walks us both quickly towards the employee parking area.

I fully expect to hear the Prospect to raise the alarm from behind us but once we get to the vehicle he was steering me towards, I realize that he still hasn't realized that I am missing so I begin to pull away from Leo's hold.

Just as I'm opening my mouth to finally scream my head off, a sharp pain flashes through my skull when Leo hits me in the side of the head with the gun in his hand.

My entire world goes dark as I realize that I'm falling towards the ground.

Leo

She really is a stupid bitch but at least she's worth a little something.

I figure I can extract most of the money I need to pay back what I owe from that idiot in that Club.

I've watched how he looks at her and a man that looks at a woman like that will pay his entire soul to get her back.

He won't be getting her back though.

While he's sending off that hundred grand, she will already be on her way to New Mexico and I'll be even richer for the price I'll get for her.

She's used goods so it won't be top dollar but the bitch still has a body on her even though she's popped out one kid already.

Wish I could have gotten the kid too.

The guys I'm in contact with would have paid top dollar for one so young and untouched.

I couldn't get to her though.

Her door is locked with a pass-code that changes daily as well as the door being guarded by several men at all times from that club.

I'll just take what I can get from Autumn.

It'll be enough to last me for a while.

I may even leave the country myself for a bit.

I heard they had some high stakes South of the border that could set me up for life if I play the cards right.

Smiling at the prone woman laying on the bed that hasn't woken up yet, I take her cell phone and take a picture.

Pulling up the man she's been staying with, I fire off a fast text with the picture demanding he send a hundred thousand dollars to a bank account at an offshore bank.

When that deposit gets posted, I'll leave Autumn at an unspecified location.

Once I'm clear of said location, I'll send him a new text letting him know where to find her.

I laugh at the screen knowing that neither of us will be anywhere near the location I send to him.

As soon as her phone says the message was read, I turn the phone off and drop it into the toilet.

With a huge grin, I pick up my own phone and send a message to verify what time I should meet my associates at the little airstrip outside of town.

Sticking my phone back into my pocket, I turn back to the woman lying on the bed.

I briefly consider taking her jacket off before doing what I have to do but decide to leave it on her.

No sense in making her sick before getting paid for her ass.

With duct tape, I tie her feet and arms before throwing her back over my shoulder and heading for the door.

Fang

Looking down at the message on my phone for the hundredth time, I squeeze it until the screen cracks.

"Focus, Fang!" Prez demands, drawing my attention in the middle of the chaos of the Club.

All of the Brother's were already mobilizing when I received the text message that Leo sent to me from Autumn's phone.

The prospect that was with Autumn noticed something was wrong when she didn't come back from getting her lunch tray.

There was really only five minutes between when he saw her last and when he got up to find her.

Not seeing her in the cafeteria, he called the other prospect up stairs to see if she went back to Olivia's room.

When he was told she hadn't returned there, he immediately called the Prez who started calling all the guys in.

Sprocket and Gear were immediately sent to the hospital to back up the prospects in case it was needed to keep Olivia safe.

"Did you give her the new key?" Snake asks quickly, booting up his laptop.

"Yeah, I don't know if she has it on her though."

Prez and I move to stand behind Snake as he pulls up the new advanced app that is connected to all the tracking devices that belong to the club.

Within a few seconds, the app pulls up a map that currently shows quite a few blue dots moving around town.

"Let me pinpoint which one belongs to her." He talks as he types.

The map moves slightly outside of town and the dot it is focusing on is moving towards the little airstrip outside of town.

The same one the club uses frequently.

"They're headed to the airport."

My heart beats rapidly, afraid of not getting to her in time.

"Blood!" Prez yells, getting his attention. "Didn't Fiona say that her brother-in-law and his new wife were coming in on a flight today?"

"Yeah. I can't remember what time though." He answers.

"Call Baratta and fill him in on the situation. See if he can contact his brother." Prez orders and Blood quickly dials his phone.

"If Giovanni can cut him off, it can give us time to get there. He'd never suspect anyone outside of the club." Prez says and I nod in agreement.

"Gio just landed. Baratta will fill him in on his way there." Blood yells out a few minutes later.

"Baratta's coming too?" I ask.

"He said he wasn't leaving all the fun to us." Blood shrugs with a grin.

"Just remember that Tony wants this guy alive." Prez says as we head out the door.

"Barely alive is still technically alive." I announce and the guys around me laugh.

I be damned if that mother fucker leave my presence without any blood being spilled first.

He touched what no longer belonged to him. He touched what was mine. He touched the woman that owns my body, heart and soul.

He has to pay for that.

Giovanni

"What now?" Raven demands from behind me.

Looking back at her, my mouth twitches with a smile.

She has her shoulders thrown back with her hands on her hip and her right brow arched up.

It's a look I know well but also one that I currently don't have time for.

"I need to take care of something but I need you to stay here. On the plane. Until I come back for you."

Her stance relaxes somewhat but she still looks at me with a serious expression.

"Are we in danger?" She asks, trying to hide the crack in her voice.

I smile warmly at her, pulling her into my arms.

"No. We are not in danger but someone else is. The Wolfsbane Ridge guys need my help."

She quickly looks towards the window as she pulls away from me.

"Who's in danger?" She asks as I move to take my case down from the storage above our seat.

Traveling by private plane sure makes it a lot easier to transport my favorite weapons.

"One of the guys' Ole Ladies." I pronounce the last bit very carefully so that I am saying it correctly.

"So one of the wives."

"I don't think she's a wife yet but the guy, Fang is his name, wants her to be. This is what Baratta told me. I need to go. Stay here, yeah?" I look over at her.

She smiles beautifully back at me and I can't stop myself from kissing her sweet mouth before heading out the door with strict instructions to the pilot to not let anyone in until I return.

Hiding my weapon under my jacket in my breast holster, I close my jacket quickly and head towards the hanger.

It's the best place to begin my search for a man with a woman that looks like she doesn't want to be with him.

I actually spot them immediately as I walk inside.

He's holding her arm tightly, dragging her with him everywhere he goes barking out orders to a rough looking bunch of assholes.

Assholes that look way too familiar to me.

Ducking back behind a pallet of boxes, I peer out at the men, scanning my brain for how I know them.

If I know them, then they will certainly know me and I'm not the type to run in without thinking it all out first.

"We need to get into the fucking air!" Leo yells.

"When we get clearance you stupid fuck! There's still a plane out there in the way!" One of the men yells back.

I grin to myself. It's my plane that is in the way and the tower won't give them clearance to leave anyway since I know that Timber, the President of the Wolfsbane MC called in a favor.

I catch movement out of the corner of my eye and I look up spotting my brother, Baratta in the rafters above.

Signaling to Baratta that he should take out the two in the back and I'll take the other two, we both lift our guns at the same time.

I know there's a chance that Leo will run with Autumn in tow but the Club should be pulling up right about now.

Giving the signal, Baratta and I pop off two shots each at the same time.

Autumn screams with the first shot and Leo pulls her in front of him, running backwards to the back door.

I hear the rumble of bikes outside so I don't bother chasing after Leo.

Instead I walk over to the four men we just put down, finding one still breathing.

Kneeling down, I look at him closely and realize exactly where I know him from.

"Should have stayed down South. Where is your boss these days? Is he still down in Cabo or has he made the same mistake as you by coming here?" I ask politely but have to move back quickly when he tries to spit on me.

"Fuck you!" He groans. Blood slowly leaking from his mouth.

He only has minutes, if that, left of this life.

I smile as I just stand there watching the light fade from his eyes.

These mother fuckers are a plague on society. They are the lowest of the low.

Kidnapping women and even children to sell them to even more sick fucks that will either use them as servants, sex slaves or just torture them for fun.

Once his breathing stops, I head towards the back door to see where everyone else is at.

We need someone to help clean up this mess.

Fang

We are just walking up to the backdoor of the hanger when we hear shots.

Grabbing our own guns, we wait only a few seconds when the door bursts open on its own.

Leo is coming out backwards, not looking behind him. He must have been trying to use Autumn as a shield from the gunfire.

Moving before he knows we are there, Blade clocks him over the head as I grab hold of Autumn, jerking her to me.

She immediately screams, not yet realizing who we are.

"It's me! It's me, baby. You're okay now."

Hearing my voice, she stops screaming and looks up into my eyes before throwing herself into me.

I hold her tightly, watching as my brothers tie up Leo and throw him into the back of one of our SUV's.

"I want him in the shed." I say out loud, drawing everyone's attention.

Blade looks to the Prez who nods his agreement.

That mother fucker is going to pay in blood for touching what is mine before I bury his ass six feet deep.

"Let's get you home beautiful." I murmur to Autumn who still hasn't let go.

"Livie?" She asks in a small voice.

"She's fine. She doesn't even know what has happened. Sprocket and Gear told her that I needed you to pick me up because I had a flat."

Pulling back from my shoulder, she looks at me with raised brows.

"You really think for one second that she believed that?" She asks.

Thinking it over until we get into my jeep, I start laughing.

"No. I don't think she believed it for a second."

I'll always have to be extremely careful where Olivia is concerned. She's far too smart for such a young girl.

One day she'll be a grown woman. Pair that with her intelligence and she'll be unstoppable.

Surely that can't be a completely bad thing. Can it?

"She'll have questions." Autumn says quietly from the passenger side.

"About her dad." I feel a small pain close to my heart.

Will she hate me if she ever finds out that I killed him? Because I do plan to kill him.

"About a lot of things. What did you mean about taking him to the shed?" She looks over at me.

I open my mouth but shut it quickly, unsure of what to say.

"She won't hate you and neither will I." She interrupts my thoughts.

"What?" I ask.

"We won't hate you if you are the reason he disappears." Her eyes, full of tears.

Instead of saying anything, I grab her hand with my own, squeezing it gently.

Chapter 11
Fang

"Hey, Munchkin, we're gonna be late." I say through the closed door.

Olivia was released from the hospital a week ago.

Since then, she has spent every moment possible outside so it surprises me that she is still in her bedroom right now.

"What if they don't like me?" She says, swinging the door open widely.

"You've already met most of them and they like you just fine." I chuckle at her. "Since when do you care what other people think anyway?"

She looks up at me, turning to her bed and plopping down on it.

"I want to fit in." She shrugs.

"I'm not understanding, Munchkin. What's going on?" Concerned, I kneel down in front of her.

She looks around her room completely before looking back at me.

"How long are you letting us stay here?"

Her question catches me off guard because I want them here forever.

"Until you and your mom want to leave I guess." I feel an ache in my heart at the thought.

"What if we never want to leave?" She asks quickly, crossing her arms.

"That's good with me." I grin back.

"What if you find someone you want to marry? Have kids with?" Her voice gets small and she stares down at the carpet.

"But I've already found that." I move so that I can look directly into her eyes. "I want to marry your mom and I want you for my daughter."

"Really?" Her little voice cracks with emotion and tears roll down her cheeks.

"Absolutely. You and your mom are my miracle. I never want to be without either of you."

She launches herself into my arms and I stand up, hugging her close.

This sweet little girl has no idea how very much I love her.

"So how about it? Will you help me convince your mom to marry me and you become my daughter?" I ask her and her tiny arms tighten around my neck.

"Damn straight!" She announces, pulling back to look me in the eye.

"Olivia! Do not use that language!" Autumn says from down the hall. "I swear I will make you eat a bar of soap!"

"Sorry mommy!" She yells back as I set her on her feet.

"I don't know where you learned such things!" Autumn says, coming to the door of the bedroom.

"From Fang of course." Livie says sweetly, giggling all the way out the door.

"Hey! You can't blame me and run!"

I take off after her, mainly to avoid facing Autumn at the moment who looks ready to give me everything she's got.

No way I'm taking the blame for this one. I know exactly who I need to have a talk with though.

Sprocket and Gear. The two shitheads with bad mouths.

Autumn

I watch as Olivia runs around playing with all the other children in the yard.

It feels so wonderful to see her being a kid again. Full of life and not so sick that she can't move.

I wouldn't have this right now if it wasn't for Fang.

Looking over at him, I catch him staring with a goofy looking grin.

"What is it? I have food on my face or something?" I ask.

Shaking his head, he leans closer to whisper in my ear.

"I love you." he says, leaning back to look at my face which I know is full of shock.

"Do you love me, Autumn?" He asks, still smiling.

That's something I don't even have to think about. "Yes." I answer.

"Then say it back. Please." He chuckles.

"I love you." I finally smile back.

"Good."

He sticks his hand into his pocket and pulls out another small box very similar to the one he gave me the key in.

Taking my hand, he places it in my palm, opening it up. I gasp in surprise.

"I want you to marry me. I want you to do so because you love me and because I love you. I also love Livie.

I told Prez a couple of weeks ago that even if I had made her myself, I couldn't have made a little girl more like me.

She is already my daughter in my heart just as you are already my wife in my heart. I just want to make it official by putting it in writing."

Tears fall freely from my eyes. I've never heard anything more beautiful said to me directly. Not ever.

"Oh, for God's sake mom! Answer the man already!"

Olivia yells and I look over to see that she's not the only one staring in our direction with a huge smile.

She evidently already knew he was planning to ask.

Figures he'd let her in on it considering just how close they are.

Two peas in a pod. Just like any other father and daughter.

She absolutely loves having a dad around and he is definitely that for her.

He's her dad in every way that truly counts.

Looking back at Fang, I wipe the tears from my cheeks with a huge grin. "Yes! I'll marry you!"

Everyone begins clapping as Fang drags me to him, kissing the breath out of me.

This man was the miracle that we needed in our lives.

In more ways than one. I can't wait to see what our future will bring.

This is Not Really the End. These boys will be back!
Read on for sneak peaks of new and upcoming releases...

The Company Book 1
Giovanni
Chapter 1

Walking into the cafe, I take a seat in the back, facing the door. It's the best way to not be caught unaware.

I'm only in town to gather Intel on a certain congressman for my employers. It seems he made them some promises that they intend for him to keep. No matter the cost.

"Can I take your order?" I turn to the voice and see the most beautiful woman I've ever seen. My eyes rake over her slowly.

"Coffee. Black." I murmur, not taking my eyes off of her even as she walks away.

What the fuck is wrong with me? I've seen beautiful women before.

Putting it out of my mind, I pull out my phone to send in an update, not bothering to look up when the waitress brings my coffee, setting it in front of me.

Her sweet smelling perfume seems to linger in the air around me. Looking up, I watch as she moves around from table to table taking orders.

She smiles at everyone politely but I notice it never reaches her eyes. No one else seems to notice the emptiness behind those dark eyes.

My phone pings telling me that the congressman is on the move. I toss a twenty on the table and head for the door.

Looking back one last time through the window, I catch sight of the waitress picking up the money with a smile that this time reaches her eyes.

Something jolts inside of me at the sight. I zero in on her name tag. Raven. The name seems to fit her perfectly.

Deciding right then, that I'll come back later to eat again even though as a rule I never return to the same place in such a short amount of time.

It's how I manage to stay under the radar. To not get caught. I'm not a good man by society's standards. I do the jobs that keep others' hands clean.

There is not a single government on this planet that is not bought and paid for in blood. If I'm ever caught, the government I work for would deny ever knowing me.

Following the tracker on my phone to a warehouse, I sneak in through a window, moving silently towards the voices that I hear in a heated discussion.

Getting into position so that I can listen in, I set up my enhanced recording device to pick up everything they say.

By the end of the impromptu meeting, I'm sure that I have more than enough for my employer to get what he wants from the congressman.

Three days later, I still haven't left town. Something about the little Raven at the cafe keeps drawing me back.

I've pretty much eaten every meal there. The truly crazy part? The woman never seems to be off work. I thought places like this did shifts that were split between all the employees yet she's here through every one of them, working the tables and sometimes helping out in the kitchen.

She's tried to engage in conversation with me on several occasions but I never answer with more than a yes or no.

While I've been studying her, I've noticed that she's started studying me. It's almost like she's not sure if she should run.

She's gotten more nervous around me as the days have passed. She spilled my coffee when filling my cup a few minutes ago.

I want to ask her what has her wound so tight that she looks ready to break but I keep my silence.

She's become an obsession that I don't need. I've already been called in for another job that I need to get to but I've put them off for now.

"I have to take the garbage out back. We'll be closing soon. Will you be okay out here by yourself for a few minutes?" I hear Raven's sweet voice ask from the counter.

Looking up into her eyes, she gets a deer in headlights look on her face. So, she feels something too? That's interesting.

"Yes. I'm going to finish my coffee." I say.

She stands there until I look away, breaking our connection. The small smile on my mouth feels foreign but I think I like it.

Raven

My heart races as I lean against the kitchen sink trying to catch my breath as if I've been running. Which is funny, because I have been running in a way.

That man just makes my nerves stand at attention for some reason. When he first started coming in for every single meal, I got nervous that they had found me again.

I'd rather die than to go back to a life where I would be expected to spread my legs for that sick fuck to plant his demon seed.

I got lucky that one of my dad's bodyguards made it out of the fire and got to me in time to save me at the cost of his own life. Now, I'm truly alone in the world. I only have myself to get me out of any danger.

I have to keep my eyes open at all times for the first sign that they have found me. It's best to not stay in one place too long. I've already been here longer than I wanted to be.

The boss man will pay my wages in two more days. I'll pack now and leave as soon as I get my money.

There has to be somewhere I can go and never be found. I'm so tired of running.

Throwing the trash in the dumpster, I go back through the back door making sure to lock it behind me.

I was so distracted; I didn't realize I walked out there without looking around first. Fuck! I'm slacking! It's definitely time to leave.

Walking back into the cafe I hear the handsome man at the counter waiting to pay his bill. He's the last customer of the night.

I've gotten used to him staying literally until I lock the doors. I'm not sure where he goes as I'm locking up but by the time I turn around he's nowhere to be seen. Almost like a ghost disappearing into thin air.

"Keep the change Raven." His deep accented voice says as he lays a twenty on the counter.

"Well, that's not fair." I say.

"What?" He stops to ask. I really expected him to do like any other time that I've tried to talk to him.

"You know my name but I don't know yours. I think that's not really fair considering you give me a nineteen dollar tip every single time you come in here." I look him straight in the eye and hold my breath waiting for him to say something else.

"Gio." He says.

"Joe? Your name is Joe?" That name just doesn't go with this man.

"No. Gio. It's short for Giovanni." He answers, holding the door open for me as we walk out, turning off the lights.

"It's really nice to meet you Gio. Did you just move here?" I ask, concentrating on locking the doors.

When he doesn't answer, I turn around and see that yet again he is gone. Like a vision that was never really there.

Shrugging my shoulders, I take off at a brisk walk towards my apartment. It's time to start packing.

Order Today:
https://books2read.com/GiovannisObsession

Night Howler's MC
Book 2
Grease

Watching my President of the club get married earlier to the woman he loves actually puts a smile on my face. Something that rarely happens these days.

I figure my marrying days have long since passed since I am turning forty-two this year. I am always too busy with work and helping to change the club over to more legal activities.

No one would want an old fucker like me anyways. I can't even imagine having kids now. Hell, I would be almost sixty before they got grown.

However, that doesn't mean that I don't still love a good romp in the sheets with a beautiful woman.

Walking around the reception at the clubhouse, I've spotted the one I want to hear screaming my name later.

She's fucking gorgeous in that simple way women sometimes have. I don't think she's even wearing makeup which in my opinion is a good thing. Most these women gob that shit on like a mask, so when you wake up next to them in the morning light you are asking yourself what the fuck you were thinking.

She has long gorgeous red hair that shines in the sunlight. She must have come straight here from work, she is wearing scrubs with a name tag.

She's currently talking to Jade who is standing next to Reaper, so I can use his ass as an excuse to get closer and at least find out her name.

As I walk up, it sounds like they are talking about Cole so this chick must work at the clinic where Jade takes the kids for check-ups.

Her eyes look over at me and then away before returning again. I give her my best smile as I look her up and down until Reaper elbows me in the ribs.

"Don't worry Britni, he may look intimidating but he's just a big teddy bear." Jade says while looking at me with slitted eyes.

"Name's Grease." I hold my hand out to her in which she takes it.

Her hands are soft just as I knew they would be from working in a doctor's office.

"Britni. It's nice to meet you." She introduces herself before pulling her hand away again.

I'm a little surprised to realize I miss the feeling of it in my own.

Britni

Coming to Jade's wedding and reception, I wasn't sure what to expect. We have all heard the rumors that circle around the Night Howler's club but I had promised I would be here as soon as I could get off work.

Jade and I became friends after she started bringing the kids into the clinic where I work. She's such a great mom to her kids I figured the club couldn't be that bad.

Everything was beautiful during the wedding and all the guys were very respectful towards me. It wasn't until I met Grease that I felt uncomfortable.

He looked at me as if he could already see my naked body underneath my scrubs. The feeling of his rough hand in my own when we met, sent chill bumps down my body causing my nipples to tingle.

He might be a little older than me but the man was hot as sin with eyes that made it even more scorching hot outside.

Even after talking to Jade while he just stood there staring at me, I could still feel his eyes on me as I walked around talking to the others.

I'm standing at the table to get a drink when I feel a body push into me from behind. I seem to already know who it is.

"Just grabbing a beer darling." He murmurs next to my ear, reaching across the table to grab a cold one from the iced down tub.

Not saying a word, I turn my head to look directly into his eyes. My breathing picks up and my body stands to attention as it notices the hardness of his pressing even more into me from behind.

Feeling bold. I press back into him with a small smile, lifting my eyebrow.

"How about we go somewhere a little more quiet so that I can hear every sigh that escapes that beautiful mouth before you scream my name." He whispers, running his tongue along the shell of my ear.

"Yes." Is all I breath out before he grabs my hand and pulls me with him across the yard stopping next to a huge bike.

Holding out a helmet, he waits to see if I take it before climbing on.

"Have you ever ridden before?" He asks.

"Not a bike." I state with a smile that makes him grin.

"Just climb on, put your feet on the pegs there and hold on tight." He grins back.

I put the helmet on and climb on, wrapping my arms around his waist. In just a few more minutes, we are flying down the road and I am loving every second of it.

Order Today:
https://books2read.com/Grease

Join Marissa Online

Website: authormarissaann.com
Facebook: MarissaAnnAuthor
Twitter: marissaannbooks
Instagram: authormarissaann
TikTok: @authormarissaann

Read More of Marissa's Books

Timber's Fairy
Blade's Pixie
Blood's Angel
Wrench's Salvation
Bear's Saviour
Torque's Gaze
Fang's Miracle
Reaper's Jewels
Grease
Buzz
Skeeter
Giovanni's Obsession
All I've Got
Baratta's Darkness
Lily's Shadow
Arin's Light
Mika's Heart
Cass' Vow
Shelby's Secret

Printed in Great Britain
by Amazon

14121197R00089